Unmaking Grace

By Barbara Boswell

CATALYST PRESS

Pacifica, California

D0052699

In North America, this book is distributed by
Consortium Book Sales & Distribution, a division of Ingram.
Phone: 612/746-2600
cbsdinfo@ingramcontent.com
www.cbsd.com

Originally published by Modjaji Books
in South Africa under the title Grace.

FIRST EDITION
10 9 8 7 6 5 4 3 2 1

Library of Congress Control Number: 2019944721

For Nina and Jesse.

A NOTE FROM THE AUTHOR

The term "coloured" in South Africa is an apartheid racial category, passed into law by the apartheid government via legislation such as the Population Registration Act of 1950. This law produced a "coloured" race, which determined where people so classified could live, work, attend school; who they could have intimate relationships with; and who they were allowed to marry. The category "coloured" remains contested in South Africa, and coloured people are often mistakenly thought of as "mixed race." However, "coloured" is more of a creole identity, described by race scholar Zimitri Erasmus as "comprising detailed bodies of knowledge, specific cultural practices, memories, rituals and modes of being" (*Coloured by History, Shaped by Place: New Perspectives on Coloured Identites in Cape Town*, 2001: 21). Those classified "coloured" by the apartheid government include a hybrid mix of the descendants of indigenous South Africans; descendants of enslaved people from Malaysia, Indonesia, Madagascar, and other Asian territories; and descendants of Dutch and British colonizers not designated "White" under apartheid. After the end of formal apartheid, some people classified "coloured" have continued to use this term to describe themselves. However, many others have rejected the term as a marker of identity.

◆

A NOTE FROM THE PUBLISHER

Though we use American spellings in this book, including for the word "color," we have chosen to keep "coloured" spelled the South African way in this novel when referring to people who go by the contested identity of "coloured." We are keeping it lower-case to indicate its un-official, contested, but common usage.

Saturn Street

Her whole life, it had been drummed into Grace that every living thing had its cross to bear and no matter how hard she tried to shake it, the house on Saturn Street was her cross. Although she'd left home at fourteen, it was always with her. It didn't matter what she did to banish it or lay it to rest, it was there; constant as the rise and fall of her breath or the steady, rhythmic beat of her pulse. Not large or small; neither looming nor ominous. Just there, like the scar on her left wrist she fingered every night as she drifted into sleep or the mole on the side of her face, part of the geography of skin. Some days it poked and taunted her, and some days it was a light cloud floating above, invisible to all but Grace, but always, always present.

On winter nights, when the cold that had gathered all day long in the crevices of the bedroom came rushing out, she would find herself returning to the place, a ghost haunting the past. On these nights, no matter how she tried to shake it—looking into the now in the mirror to solidify herself in the present—the house would come at her with a force that threatened to knock her off her feet. She'd open another bottle of wine and, alone, drain it, to stave off the memories tumbling from behind the simple brick facade. And she'd tilt into the past, still enraptured by the special brand of pain that lurked behind those long-abandoned walls. On such nights, distance and time dissolved; the now became muddied with the murky ink of the past, and it was as if she'd never left.

Grace saw Mama again, a small smile flitting about the corners of her mouth. Mama—lost in that faraway world, pondering some private joke or doing her hair and makeup. Suspended in youth, about Grace's age now: happy, glowing, alive. At other times, she flew back to the house to find Mama petrified, immobile with fear, like that night he came knocking, the night that marked the beginning of the end.

Part 1
1985

Chapter 1

"Mary, please open the door."

His voice echoed from behind the locked front door, plaintive, lost—the voice of a man adrift. "Please, my darling, just open the door, one more time. Let me in for five minutes. I just want to talk."

He sounded close to breaking. His careless confidence had deserted him. Gone was the aura of certainty that came with the knowledge that as he had ordained it, so it would be; that here, in his personal universe, he was king. All of that God-ness in him just gone. Here he was, locked out of his own home, reduced to begging to reenter his kingdom.

And just when Grace, cozily ensconced inside the house with her mother Mary, thought he could go no lower in this self-abasement, the voice rose again, soft and pliant: "Mary, Mary...I am begging you...."

In the warmth of the living room the two of them sat quietly. Grace looked back and forth from her mother's face—clenched jaw, flared nostrils—to the front door. The end of the day silhouetted her father in slanting rays of light as he paced the tiny front stoep just outside the door. Through the speckled glass his shape shifted, diffused and distorted, his body a blur, at odds with the pleading voice rising through the keyhole. Through the frosted glass panes of the door, he was somehow insubstantial—more apparition than man. Grace shivered as she took in his form.

The divorce was made final yesterday. He hadn't been living with them for a while, but just as Mama had predicted, the end of everything had sparked a new fight in him. Until yesterday, Patrick had believed Mary would take him back, as she always did after he'd performed a suitable penance. A lengthy act of contrition followed by a persistent, enthusiastic rewooing of his wife: these were the well-rehearsed steps in the dance that was their marriage. Grace had seen it many times before.

Mary had always followed where Patrick steered, leaving when she could take no more, then missing him; wavering between leaving him for good and giving him the ubiquitous last chance; basking in his renewed attention and finally succumbing to his promises. He would stop drinking, hold down a job, bring home his money on Fridays instead of spending it at the shebeen. He would go to church with them and take care of them and they'd be the family they were meant to be. Mary would believe him with a fervor that surpassed anything they'd seen in the evangelical tents that mushroomed around the place—the churches where Patrick had sought salvation and sobriety—until he lost his temper or got drunk or both, and hit her again.

But Mary, weary, had finally opted out of the dance. She had gone through with it, taken all the steps needed, and had gotten a divorce. And now here was Grace, fourteen, listening to her father begging outside. She willed her mother to keep her nerve and not reopen that door.

"Mary, I love you. Let's talk, please."

Grace wished he would shut up. Then an unexpected sympathy settled over her. If she could see him on the other side of the door, could he see them through the blurred glass? Was it cruel for her to be sitting there right across from the door, where her fuzzy outline must be visible? The red lampshade behind her cast a warm glow across the furniture. In this light, the living room seemed cozy and comfortable, not threadbare. She started to feel bad—for the warm circle of lamplight from which he had been cast but could surely see from outside, where the wind was picking up as night settled. She tried not to move, to minimize attention to herself.

Across the room, Mary stubbed out a half-smoked cigarette in an overflowing ashtray and reached for another. Her movements were sparse, just the minimum effort required to pull a fresh cigarette from its box, lift it to her lips with one hand, and light it with the other. Around her neck a gold cross glittered. Her body remained motionless, her head angled toward the door. Every fiber in her calibrated itself to the task of anticipating Patrick's next move. Mary always had an intuitive feel for when he was about to go crazy, but tonight Grace couldn't read her. Unnerved by this new paralysis in her mother, Grace closed her eyes and cloaked herself in a protective mantra. Don't open the door, don't open the door.

"Mama, why doesn't he just go?" she whispered.

Mary didn't answer. They both knew that Patrick did what he wanted, when he wanted.

"Can't we phone someone to come and make him go away?"

Mary remained quiet.

There was no one to call and they knew it. Even if there had been a police station in the area, the police were more interested in enforcing the latest State of Emergency and locking up schoolkids. Not that they'd want him locked up, not by this police. Even though Grace had heard Mary threaten to call them countless times, she knew her mother would never do it. To send Patrick straight into the hands of those who were unafraid to murder would be unforgivable.

Outside Patrick started pacing again, tracing an invisible, tightly wrought path on the small front stoep.

Again he tried. "I love you, and I'll always love you. That's all I want to say. I'll never give up on us!"

Definitive and strong: that was the father Grace knew. Through the glass his head was held high and proud. Mary must respond —a love as strong as the one he'd just declared could not go unrequited.

But in the armchair her mother remained motionless. Short puffs of smoke billowed out around her head like a halo. Her eyes were alive with a look Grace had never seen before. She was not going to answer. For the first time in her life, Mary was bowing out from her part in the choreography of his destruction. Silence settled on the room like an eternal night.

"Well, fuck you, then, Mary! Fuck you!"

The doorframe shuddered under his boot as he unleashed his fury against it, each kick punctuating the fucks flying around. A familiar knot of fear tightened Grace's stomach. "Don't think this is the last of me. Don't you dare fucking think that!"

And then he stopped. Mother and daughter exhaled. At least the door had held. Grace watched the grainy figure as he bowed down and plopped his head into his hands.

"Oh God, Mary, I'm so sorry. See what you made me do?"

The shift—the inevitable blame—fell to Mary with reassuring familiarity.

"I don't want to be like this anymore, Mary. Why didn't you just open the door?"

Tormented sobs escaped his body. Mary and Grace remained motionless throughout, frozen in fear, long past caring what the neighbors may have heard or what they might think. Grace looked at her mother with a steady gaze, willing her to stay put. For Grace, the act of contrition was always the most dangerous part of this dance. This was the moment her mother would crumble. Mary stared, unblinking, as her left hand delved for another cigarette in the little white box. She lit it, inhaled deeply, and exhaled the smoke in a sharp arrow. Her eyes lingered on Grace but looked right through her.

The sun's rays, which had allowed them to track Patrick's movements, slowly died and gave way to night. Darkness brooded around the house, pressing its face up against the big front windows where the curtains were not yet drawn. Grace could no longer see Patrick through the glass, but soft sobs confirmed his presence on the stoep. They dared not move, not yet.

After minutes that seemed like hours, the sobs faded to nothing. Yet another eternity passed before they heard the short, scraping noises of his footfall receding into the night. Mary and Grace sat together in silence for a while longer in the dark living room. When they were sure he'd left, Mary released a long sigh and crushed the empty cigarette box with her hands. She lifted herself out of the old white chair and briskly drew the curtains. After shuffling down the long, wooden-floored passage, she turned once to look at her daughter as if to say something, but then retreated into her bedroom.

Grace stood in the dark hallway, wondering if her mother would reappear to at least say goodnight. Seconds later, the shard of light underneath Mary's bedroom door died down. Grace stood for a while, a cavernous loneliness spreading through her chest. She wanted to feel her mother's arms around her. Instead, she went into the kitchen and made a peanut butter sandwich, which she ate over the sink.

In the quiet house, she padded on her white socks to the bathroom and brushed her teeth, checked that all the lights were out and all the windows closed, and crawled into bed, still wearing her blue school uniform with the red piping. Next to her, a little bedside lamp stayed on through the night to keep some of the house's darkness at bay.

Chapter 2

Patrick crouched down outside the door, defeated. He was not a man who cried, but the anger had tugged at his core until a silent, unknown part of him dislodged and spilled out in an embarrassment of sobs. Hunched forward, rocking on his haunches, he succumbed to the tears he had tried hard to stop from coming. Why had he kicked the door? He'd come here with good intentions: to talk, sit down like a reasonable man, make it right with Mary. He knew he was wrong, knew things could not go on like this. He had rehearsed the sequence of supplication, earnest declaration of change, and grateful relief to be given another chance. Yes, the divorce was now final, but papers are just that. Could a piece of paper dictate the stirrings of a heart? Could the simple stroke of a pen render love obsolete?

He didn't think so. He knew his wife well, better than anybody. He was certain that if he saw her he'd be able to talk his way back into her affections, make her see that he really knew how wrong he'd been. She'd see in his eyes that he wanted to make things right, wanted to leave all of the old ways behind this time. He would come back to his family. A fresh beginning awaited them all in this dreary old house. He would paint it, fix it up; maybe even buy the new lounge suite Mary always wanted with the money he'd save. Everything could be remade anew.

But Mary wouldn't open the door. There he was, at the threshold of a new life. She had it within her power to open up, invite him back in to find a new rhythm, but she had refused. He knew instantly, from the hollow reverberation of his voice into the unfamiliar emptiness that was his house, that something big had shifted within her. He knew she was inside, could sense her, smell her; but there was something between them not even his sweetest pleas could soften. From outside the door he saw no movement. Her silence, her not even bothering to chase him away, was more ominous than any threat or argument she could spew.

There had, of course, been lots of talks during the separation. He understood that her leaving was necessary, respected it even. He had been wrong. Repeatedly. Driven by a subterranean force he barely understood himself, he had hurt and humiliated her beyond the bounds of even his scant personal code. Early in life he had decided that morality was a ruse inflicted by those in charge—and it mattered little what they held sway over—to stay in charge. Rules, whether they were the laws of the country or the sacred covenant of marriage, were to be obeyed only to avoid punishment. Flouting rules and getting away with it, stirred in him a defiant pleasure. He took a perverse pride in his ability to belch a fearless "fuck you" into the face of the establishment. Sometimes that face was Mary's.

If he were to sit down and think about it, he might have found that beside that impulse to defy, there was also an inner voice so faint it was almost inaudible. If he'd been able to hear that voice, kept still enough to heed it, he would have found in his nature a simple moral code waiting to be lived: do unto others, protect the weak, grab joy where it's offered and give it in return. But life had deafened this voice.

He'd heard its echo when they'd met. He recalled seeing Mary that first time. Him, walking through a soft drizzle to his aunt's house where the family was gathering for Sunday tea, soaked by a sudden cloudburst just a few steps away from her door. Rain had built up from a trickle to a sluice, and icy sheets sliced into him, filling his eyes and slanting the houses crouched in his vision. He reached the veranda of his aunt's house, head down. Then, as abruptly as it had started, the rain stopped, and looking up, his eyes, still smarting from the rain, met hers.

Mary. Flying black tendrils etched against the stark white of Aunt Lydia's house. Black eyes, two large pools of darkness, made even darker by the drab Cape winter. Skin the color of milky tea. A dark, tailored jacket covering a white ruffled blouse buttoned to the throat.

Him. Suddenly at a loss for words, looking down at his shoes, saying a silent prayer of thanks that he'd polished them that morning before church. Him. Looking up into those unwavering eyes shining like coal, drawn by a magnet out of his carefully constructed self. A memory fluttered to the surface of his consciousness and retreated, stillborn. He had an odd sensation of recognition, an echo reverberating from another place or time; yet he knew he'd never seen these features before. He stood staring at her while rivulets of rain streamed down his face and body. Had she seen him running? Had he looked a fool, losing composure by running from a bit of rain? He felt embarrassed, vulnerable in front of the piercing eyes that saw everything but gave nothing.

"Good afternoon, Miss." He stretched out a hand, hoping his voice, at least, sounded firm.

"Hello," she replied.

Her arms remained folded around her slight body. He returned his untouched hand to his side.

"I'm Patrick de Leeuw."

"Mary. Pleasure to meet you." Her voice was cool as rain.

"Shouldn't you be inside, drinking tea with the ladies? Why are you out here on your own, in the cold?" he asked, gaining confidence.

"Could ask the same of you," came her reply. "At least I have the sense to stay out of the rain. You should go inside and dry off." He went inside then, leaving her on the veranda. He wasn't used to women speaking to him like that. She hadn't flirted, fluttered, or acted coy. She hadn't even smiled at him.

Inside the house he greeted Aunt Lydia and the rest of the family, toweled down, and changed into one of his uncle's old shirts.

He saw her again, when he went to get tea from the dining room where the women had congregated around a groaning table. She looked up at him, eyes burning with what looked like contempt, then averted them just a second too quickly, betraying herself. Caught looking, she blushed. Patrick knew then that the inscrutable facade was just that: a face put on for the world, armor that could be dismantled with the right combination of patience and skill. Emboldened, he moved to the corner in which she was sitting, choosing a biscuit from the plate closest to her. Standing over her, he again extended his hand. "Patrick de Leeuw."

This time she'd have to reciprocate; it would show her rudeness to his entire family if she didn't shake his hand.

"I'm Mary, Mr. and Mrs. Klein's daughter." A smile tugged at the corners of her mouth.

He remembered her now, in a much younger incarnation. The gangly, morose youngest daughter—hair plaited and ribboned, clothes always a shade less pristine than those of her immaculately clad older sister, mouth that could shame a gutter. That was a few years ago. She'd been sent away somewhere, he couldn't remember the details. Now, it seemed she was back, being reintroduced to the community in a smart suit that hugged a filled-out frame, her hair in loose curls about her face, skin polished to a translucent glow.

"It's a great pleasure to meet you, Miss Klein."

His voice was low and smooth. Her hand found his as her gaze settled defiantly on his face. This time he would not look away. He would make her look away. She was a woman; she would not dare challenge him a second time. But Mary Klein didn't look sideways or down or away. She held him with eyes as steady as he wanted to hold her. Her palm burned into his. Not a single emotion stirred in her dreamless black eyes. Standing over her, anger stirred in him. He could not fathom why he was so moved by this girl. Her thin smile now seemed to be a sneer, mocking him. His grip tightened on her hand. She winced and he let go. Her spell broken, Patrick turned his back on her without a further word and left the room. The old ladies chuckled up their sleeves.

Two nights later, having first sought permission from the head of the family, Patrick presented himself at the Kleins' door. He did not own a suit, but had pressed his trousers and was wearing a crisp, starched shirt. His shoes were polished to a high gloss; his only tie was plastered straight down the middle of his proud chest. His sturdy frame filled out a borrowed blazer, only slightly mismatched in color to his pants. Patrick knew that he looked good: clean, decent, reliable, solid.

Mr. Klein welcomed him to their modest home with an offer of a drink. Patrick declined. As Mary entered the living room, ready for their evening out, she hesitated, gazing almost quizzically at him, before extending her hand in greeting. At the moment of hesitation, Patrick sensed some kind of force, a shifting, but after it melted into the next, he wasn't sure. He convinced himself that it was nothing; that he had imagined the little movement he'd seen flutter across her soul.

He took her to see a film, some cheap Western which neither of them could remember afterwards. Then they took a long, slow walk down the main road, avoiding all shortcuts. Patrick's hand rested in the crook of her elbow. When Mary stumbled, he grabbed her and steadied her. They spoke about this and that; nothing and everything. When they reached her home five minutes before she was due, Patrick knew with certainty that death would be the only force strong enough to separate them. Three months later, on Mary's eighteenth birthday, they were married.

Chapter 3

Sometimes Grace wished her father would just die. She knew it was wrong, a mortal sin to have such thoughts, but she couldn't help thinking how much easier life would be if he just got sick or had an accident or something. She tried to halt her thoughts before they formed, but her head went in that direction and she found herself cataloging the ways in which it could happen: car accident, work accident, stabbed in a fight while drunk. All of these had already happened to him, but he was still with them.

"Onkruid vergaan nooit," her mother sighed down the line to Aunty Joan after another one of his misadventures. Mama and her sister Joan spoke every day on the phone, but her aunt wasn't allowed to set foot in their house.

Grace was lying in bed, turning over her macabre catalog of possible demises in her mind, when her mother appeared with a cup of tea.

"You're awake, my girl!" Mary said, her appearance belying what had happened the night before. "Sleep okay?"

Grace nodded.

Mary flashed a bright smile, makeup flawlessly in place. For the millionth time Grace marveled at her mother's beauty, while awe's twin, disappointment, burrowed further down in her chest. Mary's looks had skipped a generation. To have a mother so beautiful and not resemble her in any way, to get so close yet to have missed out, was one of the lesser crosses Grace bore, sometimes with fortitude, other times with spite. This morning she was again awestruck at her mother's ability to paint a fresh face over her sad nighttime one with a few deft strokes of the hand. No matter what happened in her bedroom at night, Mary emerged transformed in the morning, coated with a new, resilient skin scraped from the jars on her dresser.

"Drink up your tea while it's hot."

Her morning gift, brewed to apologize for last night and to coax Grace out of bed, came in a dainty floral cup and saucer. Pretty things mattered to Mary. Something beautiful to look at or hold against your skin could get you through a lot. And though the house might be crumbling around them—paint peeling, doors broken and unhinged by drunken fists—Mary had mastered the art of carving out, in the midst of this ugliness, a personal trove of beautiful objects: a pretty tea set, a luxurious blouse, an expensive coat. Things to stroke or smell, things from which she derived a direct sensual pleasure. These were her pretty little secrets. She lied to Patrick, always, about the origins of her luxuries. A gift from her mother, or a distant aunt. Patrick would growl for days whenever something new and pretty appeared. Sometimes he'd break them in the fights that followed.

Grace straightened up and took the cup from her mother's outstretched hand. Mary had taken extra care with her appearance this morning. Pressed curls framed her face, cascading around her shoulders, and a new shade of blush warmed her cheeks. Her brown-black eyes were lined, the lids shaded just so; her lips were the right shade of peach. Mary always stressed the importance of grooming and professional looks in her line of work, especially to Patrick, when his suspicion about her dollying up poisoned the house. Hers was the steady paycheck—always larger than his, even when he had plenty of work—which kept them housed and fed when Patrick was out of work; another of Mary's sins. She was the first line of contact any customer made, one of the few coloureds behind an actual desk. Once, having locked herself out of the house, Grace had paid a surprise visit to the bank and found herself transfixed by a strangely familiar woman. It took a few seconds before she realized it was her mother. Mary had looked like a different person: light and animated, not cowed to deflect the next accusation, the next blow.

Grace sipped her tea while her mother stood over her with a faraway smile. She was already wearing her coat, with her leather handbag on her shoulder. In a few moments she'd be gone, getting on with her day in a world far away from this oppressive room.

After Mary's departure with a quick, "Be careful today," Grace lingered in bed for a few minutes. A weak sun tried to poke through the bedroom curtains while outside, the southeaster moaned in low complaint. It had been blowing for days, enough to make anyone mad. Grace pulled herself out of bed, swallowed the last bit of tea, cold now, went to the bathroom, and brushed her teeth. The sleep creases in her school uniform would straighten out in time, and the blazer would cover the stain on her chest, she told herself as she pulled on fresh socks and her scuffed Bata shoes.

In the mirror, she attempted to tame the bush of tight, frizzy curls around her head but gave up after two sweeps of the brush. A hair-band would have to do. It smoothed down the front of her hair just fine, but everything else stuck out like thatch behind it. She turned away from the mirror, unable to stand her reflection, and headed out the door.

The sun made a feeble attempt to warm the day. Grace felt hollow. She eyed the house next door. Johnny would have left for school by now. Normally he waited for her on the corner, but she had lain in too long this morning. Just as well he'd gone. She wouldn't have been able to look him in the eye after last night's commotion on their front stoep. He must have heard Patrick's outburst—all of the neighbors probably had. They were used to his drunken rages, but the children of the neighborhood never tired of mocking Grace the next day. Thank God Johnny wasn't like that. But she still couldn't bear the thought that he had heard.

As she turned the corner of Saturn Street to join Main Road, the wind unleashed its full fury. White grains of sand peppered her legs, her eyelids, the soft inside of her mouth. Pulling her blazer tight around her, Grace hunched forward, pitting herself against it. The devil was dancing in this wind; she felt it in the violent tugs. The southeaster was a male wind, it was said, always trying to lift women's skirts.

She approached the school from a side street—for weeks she had been avoiding all main roads to keep out of the way of the police. As she climbed through a hole in the fence behind the main school building, a row of armored vehicles rolled slowly down a deserted Main Road past the school's front gate. She thought about turning and running back home, but the emptiness of the house and the thought of being alone for hours propelled her across the soccer field toward the first class of the day.

The school bell whined a shrill warning as Grace ran across

the field toward the quad where students lined up before classes began. Something wasn't right. The kids were huddled in little groups. Instead of the usual lineup, they were milling around, congealing in small circles. She saw the science teacher, Mr. January, come running out of his classroom, his tie fluttering in the wind. Like a good herd dog, he tried to round up the younger children and shoo them inside. As she neared the quad, Grace saw him tugging at one of the older boys' sleeves. They tussled for a bit before Mr. January gave up, turned, and went back inside.

Mounting chaos, a frenetic energy, grabbed hold of the school. Students poured out of classrooms, like confused ants in the usually neat quad. Grace tried to make her way to her math class, wanting nothing to do with these politics, but she was jostled and pushed up against an inchoate flow of bodies. Skilled at the art of making herself invisible, she stood with her back to a wall and waited for a gap. As she passed Mr. January's classroom, she heard his low voice, gravelly from too many cigarettes and years of shouting at students, his muted plea directed at no one in particular. "God help us."

Chapter 4

Her own classroom was in disarray: no teacher present to take the register, and boys from the higher standards standing on desks and leaning out of the top windows, the only ones that could open to allow air in. There was a smattering of the usual thirty-five students in the class. In a back corner a group of girls had bunched their desks together into a protective laager. They sat nervously, clinging to each other for comfort. Grace joined them. She started to ask a question but was silenced by Lorraine, an older girl, as the group tried to catch snippets of information from words drifting down like scraps of paper on the wind from the boys, who provided a halting commentary on the activity outside.

"That one, over there! Unmarked police car."

"You can see them, the Boere!"

All week members of the Student Representative Council had been planning this protest. Grace had heard details but she'd tuned them out. There was enough going on at home. Banners had been drawn and placards prepared. The protest would be peaceful, demanding what any sane human being in this society would want: Mandela released, apartheid ended, this gutter education brought up to standard.

The message had been echoing through the courtyards, the hallways, and the classrooms for weeks.

Free Mandela! Unban the ANC! Unban the PAC! Bring our leaders back home!

Today it came from a loud-hailer in the main quad. Seated at their desks the young girls heard the protest begin.

"Let's go," said Lorraine. "Let's go join it."

"No, I don't want to get involved in this," Claire said. "My parents warned me to stay away from politics."

Grace followed the debate, not sure whose side she was on,

nor daring to insert her own voice. Always the quiet one, always going along with everyone else, she hated herself for not having an opinion and not stating it firmly like these girls could do. What would she say, anyway? She knew apartheid was wrong, but hadn't it been drummed into her at home to respect authority above all else? Challenge the rules and you could get hurt— at home or at school. She wanted to be decisive and quick, to know what she thought. Instead she just sat there watching Lorraine grab her stuff and leave while Claire's face contorted with disapproval. Two others remained with them, afraid of the wrath of the policemen lining up outside.

Outside in the quad, the student rally was hitting its stride. "Amandla!"

"Awethu!"

The crowd, growing denser by the minute, grouped around the head protesters, eager to respond to the leaders' demands. An older boy stood in the middle of a clearing of bodies, loud-hailer glued to his lips.

"We demand freedom! We, the young people, are the future of this country. We want justice! Viva the ANC, Viva!"

"Viva!" the crowd responded in unison. "Viva the PAC, Viva!"

"Viva!"

"Viva Mandela, Viva!"

"Viva!"

The crowd took over chanting: "Mandela! Mandela! Mandela!"

A tall, lanky boy, made for the role of flag bearer, waved a big green and yellow banner imprinted with Mandela's image. Grace, peeking out of the classroom door, took it in, wondering: who was this Mandela? Since the beginning of the year his name had hummed beneath the surface of her life at high school. They sang about him, chanted his name, demanded his freedom. He was locked up somewhere, wrongly, for wanting to end apartheid. This much she knew. Nobody knew what he looked like. His picture wasn't in any history books, newspapers, or on television. She had never heard his name spoken at home, not when the going was good between her parents, and certainly not during the bad spells. The image on the flag seemed ghostly, like the only grainy picture of a long-dead relative who had been important and influential, but who you didn't know at all. Who was this

Mandela they were shouting for, really? Would he get them the vote, get rid of apartheid and Botha, and bring peace to the troubled streets? Did he beat his wife? Or would he, if he was free to do so, if she didn't do things the way he liked?

"Mandela! Mandela!"

The chants rose up louder. The group started toyi toyi-ing to the rhythm of the freedom song, spilling out of the quad, ready to take to the streets. Banners waved furiously. Grace ached for the quiet of home, wishing she'd stayed there.

"Fok! Hier kom hulle!"

The sentries who had remained behind in her classroom jumped from the desks and ran out to warn the others of impending disaster.

"The Boere are coming!'

Grace saw Johnny in the quad. He looked her way and waved at her, mouthing, "Go!"

Another wave of boys swept down the corridor. "Out! Out! Get out!" they screamed at the petrified girls.

"Get the fuck out and run home as fast as you can! The Boere are coming!"

Claire, ever the ringleader, declared, "No, we'll do what we want!"

The group of girls, Grace included, followed her across the classroom to where some of the boys were still perched as lookouts. Grace clambered onto a desk and strained to reach the top of the window. Row upon row of armored trucks were rounding the corner of the street next to the school's front gate, helmeted soldiers protruding, guns ready. For one insensible moment they seemed to Grace like play cars, a convoy of army trucks like she'd seen the littlest kids next door push back and forth, back and forth; cute, harmless blocks of wood. Toy trucks for a staged fight, where the good always triumphed over evil, where everything was cleaned up and packed away afterwards and everyone went home friends. It hit Grace that the armored Casspirs were blocking off the school gate, cordoning off the way out. An unearthly ringing started in her ears, and unable to stir or look away from the approaching Casspirs, her limbs went limp.

Then, suddenly, Grace was moving fast, out of the classroom as if winged, her feet barely touching the ground. Johnny must have come running up the stairs to fetch her. He had her by the collar of her blazer and was hustling her onward, out, out. In the quad, they stopped to hear the soldiers, with loudspeakers ten times more powerful than the students', command: "You have five minutes to disperse! Five minutes!"

From every direction, children poured into the quad. Like sheep rounded up by an unseen herd dog, bodies ran, walked, churned against each other, not knowing whether to go or stay, not knowing how to leave. Mindful of a stampede, the leaders tried to induce some order. The teachers were nowhere.

Then: shots. One, two, three. A shooting star hung briefly suspended above them before landing in their midst, unleashing its poison. A small dust cloud bloomed into full evil, and Grace knew in that instant that she was going to die. The gas ripped into her, into the delicate tissues of nose, eyes, and mouth. The top layer of her skin was being eaten away. She couldn't breathe. Tried to cough. Gasped for air but swallowed fire. Throat melting, eyes burning out of her head, she could not see a thing. She was aware of only the burning, burning.

She started moving again, without volition, amidst the sea of bodies being swept out by a current to God knew where. In the press of bodies the students rounded a corner out of the quad and then Grace was breathing again, her lungs greedily sucking the air. She felt a hand at her back: Johnny's, pushing her away from the main school building.

"Run, run! Go to the hole in the fence. Run home!"

Lungs still burning, Grace ran with a crowd of students across the soccer field toward the makeshift exit in the school fence, but the soldiers, guessing their escape plan, rolled in their Casspirs toward it, rifles ready. Fear became the fire in her throat, the burning of her insides, the liquid running down between her legs.

All running together, but each alone, the students' race against the soldiers seemed futile to Grace even as she ran with the herd. There was nowhere to hide, just the soccer field with no chalked lines and browning patches. Throats on fire, they ran the length of the field, not daring to look up or back or around. Johnny had disappeared. With skin and eyes burning, tears and snot streaming down her face, Grace shot forward with the crowd.

Another dull pop echoed across the field. Another teargas

canister launched at them, thudding on the earth. Faster they ran, trying to outrun the convoy rolling toward the stream of kids congealing at the hole in the fence. Turn around or continue forward? Everyone else kept moving forward, so Grace stayed within the safety of numbers.

At the hole, the group bottlenecked. Dancing to the invisible flames of teargas, some fell, while others trampled over prostrate bodies in their haste to get through the gap that allowed passage to only one person at a time. Grace felt herself being pushed up against the fence. She managed to break free. As the stream of children halted, she took a gap and decided to leap through the fence. She was about to step through the hole when her knees collapsed and her body hit the ground. The noise of the approaching armored trucks deafened her. She felt harsh rubber soles treading into her back. Then unseen hands lifted her quickly, securely, and shoved her through the fence. She turned back for a second, expecting to see him, but there was no recognizable face, just an endless blur of children crowded at the gap.

"Move!" they chided, and Grace started running again. Students scattered in all directions as a volley of shots rang out. Grace saw a house ahead of her and she ran for it. She clambered over the low front wall and lay down behind it, hoping she was hidden. More shots rent the air. These were sharper than those that had released the teargas. She crawled around the garden keeping to the wall, then scaled an intersecting fence, dropping into the neighboring yard. Through a window, a woman her mother's age screamed, "Get out! Don't come running through my yard! Do you see me looking for trouble?"

Grace slipped through a side gate, and for the first time since the protest began, her limbs relaxed a little. A full block away from the soldiers, separated by a double row of houses, she slowed to catch her breath. Unless they jumped out of the vehicles to start chasing on foot, she was safe. She slowed down, turned, and saw a plume of smoke rising from the school grounds. The last part of her journey home was a blur. Her legs were the consistency of rubber by the time she reached the yellow house on Saturn Street and unlocked the front door and the metal security gate. Inside, as she sank to the floor, a terrible thought screeched into consciousness. What if they'd followed her, could see her through the lace curtains? She crawled against the faded white couch and stayed there, for how long she didn't know. Waiting. Waiting. Examining the cracks in the unpolished wooden floor. Holding them with her eyes as though her life depended on it. Guarding the tiny specks of white sand, blown underneath the door by the terrible howling wind. How neatly the grains lined up against the edge of the threadbare, fraying carpet. Taking in the dirty-orange rug speckled with brown; watching where the grains of sand had settled and nested, like tiny eggs, into its fibers. Watching one ant, then another, making its way across the living room. Feeling nothing.

This was the kind of magic Grace had learned in this house. How fixing your eyes on one thing, just one little thing—say a crack in the wall—could make everything else disappear: your parents, their shouting, the wind, the snap of fist upon flesh. The sound of Casspirs circling, the fevered cries outside, her limbs, her own body—none of these existed after Grace tuned them out. She became a mind, a pure mind, floating on the thing she'd chosen to fix on. She could project her entire being on that crack in the wall, that speck of white sand. It held her. It got her through whatever was raging on the outside.

Mary was late from work that evening. By the time her key turned in the lock Grace had gotten off the floor, but she was sitting hunched up on the couch in the darkening living room.

"Grace! Oh, thank God!"

Mary's eyes were wild as she rushed over to her daughter and pulled her to her.

"Why haven't you switched on the lights? All I saw as I was coming up the road was darkness!"

She let go of Grace and rushed around the room again, flicking on every switch as if to ward off evil, then sat back down next to her daughter, embracing her.

"What happened today?"

"Nothing, Mama."

"Why won't you tell me?"

Mary reached into her bag, not waiting for an answer, and produced from it a box of cigarettes. She lit up and inhaled. Sitting up straight, it looked as if she was bracing herself for something.

"Grace," she said, blowing smoke at the ceiling, not looking at her, "Johnny is gone."

Her voice was soft and low. It was the same benevolent voice she used to deny Grace something she could not have.

Grace retreated deeper into silence, although her eyes searched for her mother's.

"They think the cops shot him at the school," said Mary. "They think he was helping the others to get out. No one has seen him since this afternoon. The police came out and ran into the school grounds. Did you see him? Do you know anything, Grace?"

"No."

Words were spilling out of Mary—incomprehensible, senseless words that Grace wanted to stop.

"I just came past their house. Rowena is in a state...!"

Grace fought the urge to hit her mother in the mouth in order to stop the stream of words.

"...Tim has driven everywhere, all the hospitals and police stations..."

After a waterfall of words, Mary fell quiet, staring into the distance and dragging on her cigarette, lost in her own world again. Grace wanted to scream, but the fog of cigarette smoke and silence choked her, strangling any sound. Instead, she looked at her fingernails, inspecting the arch of the white tips against the pink nail beds and the frayed bits of cuticle sticking out of her left ring finger.

Her mother sighed, smoothed down her hair, and got up to go to the kitchen. Grace heard the lid of the kettle, a sharp stream of water, and a click of a switch. She went back to examining her nails.

Mary emerged with two cups of tea. "Drink!" she ordered.

Ever the obedient daughter, Grace did as she was told until she'd drained every drop of the strong, sweet tea.

Chapter 5

Patrick stepped off the bus and onto a burning street. Barricades of blazing tires choked Main Road as he made his way to his former home, sending plumes of black smoke into the dying day. The smell of petrol clung to the air. Flames danced from all sides of the road, making it difficult to know where to tread. He had been heading to his new place—a small bedsit tacked onto someone's house, about five minutes from the home he used to share with Mary. The bus ride home had started uneventfully, but with each new passenger the chatter grew. The children had staged a demonstration at the local high school. They were peaceful, but the police had opened fire anyway. One child, maybe two, had been shot; others were missing. Patrick listened, not daring to ask questions. Grace was fine, of that he was sure. She wouldn't be caught up in a demonstration of that sort. His daughter was far too timid a creature. She preferred to stay in the background and not be noticed.

Yet she also had a willful streak in her. Mostly she did what she was told, obeyed orders without talking back. But then, out of the blue, there'd be a day when she'd just dig her heels in, refuse. She was like Mary in that way, although not as insolent. When it happened, the child's defiance was all the more infuriating because it surprised him, coming out of nowhere as it seemed to. Like that one time she'd disappeared for half a day into the bushes near the airport. He had looked all over for her, combing the streets trying to find her—she had never ventured away from home before. Then just as the sun was setting she had reappeared, with a smirk on her face as if nothing had happened. He had not been able to control his rage. Yes, she could be defiant in the most surprising ways. But he didn't think someone with her innate fearfulness would go near such trouble as had happened at the school today.

26   **UNMAKING GRACE**

Yet, as the bus drew nearer to the township, uncertainty gnawed at him. If something had happened to Grace, he would surely have heard by now. Mary or the principal would have called him at work, he reasoned. But he had just started this new job as a mechanic at JB's Autos, and now he couldn't remember whether he had given Mary his new phone number, what with the trouble between them.

Patrick tried to stay calm, picturing the girl safe in bed or watching television in the living room. That's probably what she was doing right now. Still a layer of sweat beaded his body. Waves of fear rose from his belly to his chest. What if the unthinkable had happened? He had already lost one child. He wouldn't be able to stand the loss of another.

He shot a little prayer heavenward. Please, God, let her be okay. Then he laughed at himself, for hadn't he long ago forsaken God? Or God forsaken him? But habits die hard. Give me a child for the first seven years of their life, and I'll give you a Catholic for the rest of their life, the brothers at school used to say, only half joking. Most of Patrick's young life had been testimony to that sentiment. By the age of ten he had been adept at leading three younger siblings to Mass each Sunday. Then there were novenas on Tuesdays, praying of the rosary Thursdays, and catechism on Sundays. He'd served as an altar boy, helped his mother when she volunteered to wash and iron the priests' robes at the local parish. He'd dutifully taken himself to confession every two weeks, making sure, in advance, to examine his heart and conscience for the tiniest speck of wrongdoing. Because sin left unchecked, even the seed of sin, destroyed lives; and he, Patrick de Leeuw, had determined from the age of reason that he would live a life worthy of redemption.

Not that he deserved redemption. He knew himself, even as a young boy, to be tarnished with the stain of sin. He was a lowly sinner like all the rest of them, but he had been taught that redemption could be found through striving for goodness and humble supplication before God. It had been drummed into him: always know that you are a sinner; never forget that. Work hard to atone for that sin. He always did. He would go to confession, determined to start anew and not sin again, as the priest exhorted.

But then the problem of sinning would creep in, again and

again. Always, even moments after atonement, the very second after the priest's absolution, he would find himself doing wrong again, or find the shadow of a bad thought flitting through his mind. He would be stained and dirty again. He would feel guilt and remorse, and the priest's confessional would not be close enough to absolve him as quickly as he needed. The maintenance of a state of sinlessness became increasingly difficult. And then the thing at school happened, and he'd been so sullied that he could never again think of himself as clean, sinless, again. Certain sins could not be forgiven, especially if one had willingly participated in them. At the age of fifteen, God left him, and Patrick gave up trying to find him again.

For a year afterwards, his torment knew no bounds. Although he was keeping up the dizzying cycle of pretense—daily Mass, Sunday Mass, novenas, confession—he knew in his heart that he was not good enough for God, would never be good enough. It didn't matter that he tried. Wracked with anguish, Patrick tried to imagine the life, and afterlife, that lay before him. Damnation, eternal damnation awaited him. Contemplating his fate, the fear of God became permeated with a slow-rising anger. Why would God have created him this way—stained and flawed—knowing full well that the attainment of purity would never be his? And why had God let these things happen to him? Was his life a cruel joke, and did God watch on in amusement as he strove and failed in an endless, agonizing cycle? Was that God? If it was, then he wanted no part of God. Fuck that. This decision relieved him.

And so he came to take pleasure in his sinfulness, enjoying his willful defiance. He wallowed in his soul's squalor and found a deep satisfaction in examining the many facets of his wrongdoing, flaunting them in the world's face. Fuck you, church, and fuck you, God! He took up drinking, grew to enjoy it. Yet even in his most drunken excess, a kernel of fear remained. It was there, worrying him, like a tiny grain of sand in his shoe, a dull undercurrent to his life and pleasures. God was watching, waiting. Although he had turned his back on God many times, the knowledge of a supreme being watching his every move had never really left him. Recently he had tried going to the big evangelical tents. They were so different, much happier. He had even gotten baptized, but deep inside, couldn't shake the feeling that he was faking it. God was really hollow; you could make him anything you wanted him to be. Patrick had never felt his presence.

But at times like these—where was the girl?—he still went to God, like an addict reaching for a fix, and prayed like a child with blind belief. Did God ever answer him? He couldn't say. For years he'd had Mary. Some would have called her a prayer answered. But the impulse to do things he knew was wrong, the vertiginous pull of pleasure, was often stronger than his love for her.

He was twenty-one when they'd married, determined that his life would be different from the one he'd known growing up in the cramped street where everyone knew each other's business. He would treat her like gold, unlike the way he had seen his father treat his mother, sentencing her to an early grave. The blows he'd witnessed inflicted upon his mother had broken more than the bones in her tiny body: he had seen, along with the bruises, the destruction of her spirit, her light being snuffed out bit by bit, until there was nothing left but a shell of a woman who, at forty-five, succumbed to a stroke. The eldest child, Patrick had despised his father for what he'd done to his mother. He despised himself even more for his inability to protect her.

Things would be different with Mary. There was a sadness in her which evoked in him the urge to protect, to try again where he had failed with his mother. But Mary's sullen, hard side, her refusal to be dominated, vied with her childlike softness that so enchanted him. She could be hard to her core, capricious in her whims, fluctuating often in manner between guileless, beautiful child and bitch. She could play on his sympathies one moment, elicit cosseting and affection, and then reject him with her very next breath. Patrick wasn't always sure which Mary he'd encounter. During their short courtship, he had watched these moody fluctuations with wry amusement, indulging her as one would a spoiled child. Once they were married, he would put his foot down. It would be time for her to grow up. They'd be a family, and he'd be the head. He would be in for a bit of a time breaking her in, but no doubt he would be able to do so within a few months. Once she conformed and settled into the role of wife, he would be a good husband to her. He was not his father's son. He would be the proud head of his family, a protector and provider to Mary and the children they would have together.

Their wedding had been a small affair. Between the two families there was not much money. Mary wore a simple gown, white of course, stitched by his aunt Patricia. He was dapper in the first and only suit he would own. Standing next to her on their wedding day, his pitch black suit offset her lovely black eyes, which were darker than ever but glinting with a love he could feel when he looked into them. Till death do us part, they both said.

Had he still believed in God then? Thinking back now, he could not remember. But he had meant it when he had promised before God to love, cherish, and protect his wife. That promise meant something, if not to God, then to himself, even as Patrick remembered, in that very moment of vow-making, his proclivity toward pleasure. This he would overcome, and in loving his wife, would create for himself the life he had always craved.

Patrick had not reckoned on Mary's shameful confession in their marital bed on their wedding night. In their new closeness, and faced with a similar need to exorcise the past as she stepped into their shared life as husband and wife, Mary had unburdened herself of a deep and heavy secret.

For a few weeks after their marriage, Patrick considered a divorce. But he was a Catholic, and that would be difficult. He wished to heap no more shame on himself by exposing her past. Annulment was an option, but he had dithered too long. It was easier to remain married, but the life he had dreamed of with Mary had been destroyed.

From that day on, he could never look into those dark pools of light, which had seemed so beautiful, without seeing there the hardness of Mary's soul. Every time he looked into her eyes, he remembered what she had done. His love had been sullied. Never again would he look at her and be engulfed by the tender mixture of longing, protectiveness, and love. From then on, he could stand to look at her face for only so long. Then, sickened, he would be forced to turn away. Now those eyes mocked him, pleading with him to love but stirring only disgust.

Mary's beauty, first a source of pride, turned overnight into a torment. It enraged him. How could someone so beautiful have been capable of the thing she had done? How could her looks be so opposed to what he now knew resided in her heart? He wished he could find her ugly. But even though her soul repulsed him, her outward appearance now mesmerized him even more. Mary's physical allure grew stronger in proportion to his growing revulsion. There was an urge to possess, to own even, her past and somehow erase it. In the physical act of love, he could momentarily do so, but afterwards he would always return to the present, back to Mary and her shamefulness, her hard eyes, and he would push her away. There was no need or desire to protect her, only to possess her. And this Patrick did absolutely.

Mary could leave his sight only to go to work and church. He did not like her working, but had little choice. They had moved, after their marriage, into a new housing scheme for coloureds far outside of the city on the Cape Flats. They were not allowed to buy the property, but as renters their expenses were high and could not be met on his apprentice salary. He allowed Mary to go and work as a shop assistant in a nearby suburb. She was good at her job and soon found a better paying one at the bank. Patrick, always struggling with rules and his temper, never finished his apprenticeship as a mechanic, and he drifted from one low-paying job to another. So he allowed his wife to work, but beyond that decreed that she be home at all times. He had always been an excellent timekeeper. He knew that a trip to the nearby shops should take twenty-five minutes: five to walk there, fifteen to pick out her groceries, five to walk back home. If she exceeded those minutes, he'd be waiting for her, ready with questions. Who had she seen? He would ask her again and again, persisting, hearing, and hating how his voice dripped with a mixture of bile and jealousy. Who have you been with, this time?

It worked: he gained almost full control over her.

For the most part, he thought she had settled down, but often she was sullen and only spoke to him when he spoke to her first. In this barren new place, they knew no one. They had neighbors, but Mary didn't concern herself with them. He preferred it that way. He didn't like the idea of his wife gossiping over a fence. Sometimes when he was between jobs, he would watch her walking down Saturn Street coming home from work. She walked with her head up high and her eyes straight ahead of her. If it was cold, she would have her hands deep in the pockets of her coat. If there were people about, she did not pause or stop and speak to anyone. He could see how the neighbors looked at her as she passed, how they fell silent, their eyes appraising her, and the corners of their mouths turned down. And it was true. Mary was standoffish in nature. He had experienced it the days they first met. Some people might have seen her as a snob, with her light complexion, acting white. He could see what they were thinking. Sometimes they scoffed at her within earshot. It was better that way, Patrick thought. He did not want his family's business being talked about in strangers' living rooms anyway. For his part, Patrick wondered: what was the use? What was the fucking use of vows and promises and strivings to be good and do right by people? He had been let down.

It was easy to slip back into the old ways, find solace in the shebeens, in the drink and available bodies to be found there. As their six-month wedding anniversary passed, unmarked, he started to follow the path leading to the local shebeen the moment he stepped off the bus from work, delighting there in the distractions from his wife's beautiful, sour face. Soon he was seldom home earlier than midnight, and never sober. Mary was nearly always asleep when he got home, turned on her side in their bed, away from him.

But then she started waiting up for him. She was obviously distressed at the state he was in. He could see judgement and disgust on her face. One night she cried and put her arms out to him. She pleaded with Patrick to stop, stop his reckless be-haviour. She begged him to come back to her. She wanted her sweet Patrick back, she said, the one she had fallen in love with, the man who had her heart. "Don't speak to me about love!" he had screamed at her.

And then, one night, it happened. For the first time he had raised his fist, and with the force of close to a year's suppressed rage, smacked it against the vulnerable curve of her lip. Mary crumpled to the floor. A wave of remorse instantly swept over him. Patrick knelt down next to her, cradled her sobbing face, whispered over and over, "I'm sorry, I'm sorry. I didn't mean to do that." Gently, he lifted her from the floor and led her to their bed, where he held her until her sobs subsided and she fell asleep in his arms. The sound of her even breathing comforted him. He was struck by the realization that the protective swelling in his chest, which had fled that first night, was back. Gone was the pent-up anger he had carried in every muscle for the past months. There, in this unhappy bed, was tenderness again, an unexpected guest. He welcomed it with relief.

For a while after Patrick took care with his wife. He enveloped her with concern, and showered tenderness upon her. He came straight home from work, abandoning his nightly detours to the shebeen. And when Mary gave him the news that she was pregnant with their first child, he thought they might be a family after all. She became more relaxed, allowing her body and spirit to soften a little into his embrace.

But it didn't last. It couldn't. Some or other upset at work, or maybe an absence from home by Mary he deemed longer than necessary—he could not now remember which—and Patrick found himself back at the shebeen, buying rounds for an appreciative crowd. The anger sprouted within him again—its seed had not been eradicated—and fueled by liquor, it erupted again, each time with increased intensity.

Patrick hated the way she would drop to the floor at his first contact and roll herself into a ball, holding her arms over her growing belly, shielding herself and his baby from him as if he were a monster. It infuriated him. And when she cried or pleaded, that infuriated him more. It was better when she was in bed by the time he came home, but he could tell by her breathing when she wasn't sleeping, all tucked tight, tight with the duvet round her. He saw the swell of her belly rise and fall as she lay there. Before he knew it, his hand would shoot out and he'd see her mouth contort as a lip split. "Liar," he would whisper. "Whore. You say you care about this child? Liar!"

Soon after their first wedding anniversary, Mary gave birth to a perfect baby boy. He had the sweetest face. When Patrick entered the room where Mary was holding him and gazing down at him enraptured and overwhelmed with love, it took him a few moments to see her tears. She didn't look up at him, just kept her eyes on the tiny, unmoving, silent little bundle in her arms. Patrick did not have to move closer to know what he knew, to discover what had been given and taken at the same moment.

He stood motionless by the foot of the bed for what seemed like an eternity. Deep anguish distorted the contours of his face, but he would not allow himself to feel it. His eyes burning, mouth contorted, he looked at Mary, accusing her, hating her more than ever as tears streamed down her cheeks. "Happy?" he said. "You've killed another baby." God had punished both of them for Mary's sin.

Oh, the boy! Now, so many years later, Patrick could still see his small, serene face. The image would stay with him until he drew his last breath. He took out the precious memory of his son, the one with his nose and the curve of his mouth, almost daily, examining that cursed treasure that he couldn't let go, could not put to rest. And now, on the bus, Grace's face was somehow blurred into the image of the boy's, so that, for a moment, he could not remember the features of either of his children. My son, my son! He felt the wound again as he stepped off onto the road, fearing, this time, for Grace.

Patrick made his way through the burning barricades, hurrying straight to the house he had until recently shared with Mary and Grace. There were no cops around, thank goodness, but Patrick clenched his hand around his trusted Okapi all the same. He was not afraid to use it: anyone who thought they could mess with him would find that out. As he branched off from the main road, entering a maze of tributaries, the crowds thinned and the smell of burning petrol faded. A few meters from his old house he broke into a run. Just one more corner and he'd be there. He wanted to touch her, touch his Grace and feel her forehead, her limbs, make sure each part of her was intact. He rounded the bend and headed straight into a row of parked cars. They were outside of Tim's home. Patrick's heart stopped with fright. Something was happening here. There were too many cars, too many people milling around on a night when it would be safer to remain indoors. Not a light shone from his old home. Please God, he prayed again. Moving up to the front door, he knocked, repeating the previous night's scene. "Mary, open the door!"

He saw a faint movement behind the dappled glass. Mary was there, sitting alone in the dark again. "Mary! Where's Grace?"

Mary got up from her seat and briefly moved out of sight. Then her head appeared through a crack in the small window at the side of the house.

"She's here. She's okay. And since when did you care anyway?"

"I need to see her. Please, Mary."

"She's asleep. Go away."

The window squeezed shut. As quickly as relief washed through Patrick, rage flushed his body. Bitch! How dare she! How dare she keep him away from his child? He wanted to pump the door with his fists, but a commotion was brewing next door.

Distracted by the growing crowd, Patrick went off to hear what was happening. Johnny was missing. That was too bad—Patrick was fond of Johnny. After commiserating with the gathering, he found himself in that habit of old, saying a prayer for the boy. He asked if he could help, but no one paid him much attention, and after hanging around for a bit, feeling utterly useless, he walked slowly away into the night.

Chapter 6

He had rolled in like overnight fog off the bay. Johnny was thirteen years old when he first appeared next door, conjured like a magician's trick. Grace was eleven. He had moved in with Tim and Rowena, a couple who lived in the neighbor's garage because there was nowhere else to find safe, decent housing. They had just had a baby and then, one day, Johnny too. His arrival was not heralded, nor a happy occasion; he came and slotted right into their lives in the tiny converted structure that housed kitchen, bedroom, and living room for four. To Grace's eleven-year-old self, Johnny might as well have been thirty, so much older did he seem. His eyes had a look of having seen too much, in too short a time; his body seemed stronger and more weathered than other boys his age. There were lots of other children living in the main house and the proliferation of backyard shacks next door. Johnny was unlike them. He never ran, played, laughed, or teased. He had a seriousness about him that was beyond his years. He seemed to prefer to keep to himself.

Johnny's story spread across the fences of the township faster than a bushfire, gathering momentum and embellishment as it moved. Despite their proximity to his new home, Grace's was the last house on which the story settled. Johnny had been orphaned a few years earlier, left with only two older brothers who were already making their way in the world. The oldest had taken him in and, in his first misguided act of guardianship, had plucked Johnny out of school, setting him to work at a fruit and vegetable stand by the side of a slip road off the highway. The boy would sit there peddling his wares, from sunup to sunset, and was paid twenty-five cents per day for his labor. At home he was treated worse than the dog. His brother's wife despised him and grudgingly fed this extra mouth the family's leftover scraps. During the summer he slept on a mattress underneath the fruit and vegetable shelter in the back yard, partly to guard the wares, but mostly because his presence was unwanted in the main house. After one particularly vicious beating from his brother, Johnny ran away and drifted through the homes of a succession of distant relatives. After a few months of this, he ended up next door with Tim and Rowena. When he arrived his only possessions were a pair of shorts and the stained, yellowing shirt already on his back.

The first thing Tim and Rowena did for him was provide two new shirts and a fresh pair of trousers. The second was to enroll him in school. Although he hadn't seen the inside of a classroom for years, it was soon apparent that he had a good head on him and a curiosity which enabled him to learn fast. Johnny loved school. He loved the order of the day broken up with two lunch breaks; loved his uniform; loved his dirty old satchel and the meager books that were passed on to him. He did so well that he was allowed to skip a standard and, before very long, had almost caught up to where he should have been. And now he was gone, snatched from the place he loved by God knew who.

Sleepless in bed that night, Grace's mind was a frantic, caged animal as she searched the possibilities of where he could be, the state he might be in. She conjured his arrival in their lives, as if summoning him in that way would make him reappear in the flesh.

He was one of the few children in their neighborhood who had ventured over the fence into their yard. Mary, just home from work, was exhaling the day along with her cigarette smoke. Patrick was not yet home when they heard the timid knock on the back door. Mary, unaccustomed to guests, bristled with surprise and gestured to Grace with a sweep of the hand and a flash of panicked eyes to get the door.

"Good afternoon," said Johnny politely, staring at some point above Grace's head. "Is your mother home?"

His English was broken, not fluid, like hers. Mary had made sure she spoke only English in the house so as not to be mistaken for one of those common coloureds.

"She's not here," Grace replied.

For the first time, after weeks of peering at him through their lace curtains, Grace was able to study him up close. The hair, thick and wavy, clung in stubborn curls close to his scalp. A smattering of freckles danced across sunburned cheeks. Guarded eyes refused to meet hers, leaving Grace to contemplate thick, long lashes. An awkward silence looped between them, crackling the air. Emboldened by his shyness, his shuffling from one foot to the other, Grace felt powerful; the gatekeeper between him and what he wanted.

"Then I'll come again later," he mumbled, turning to shuffle away on cracked and dusty heels.

"What is it?"

Unbeknown to her, Mary had appeared behind Grace, and she addressed the boy sharply.

"Middag, Auntie. Auntie, can I do a little bit of work for you in the yard, pull out some plants or maybe sweep?"

Grace suppressed a laugh. Had this fool actually seen the state of their yard, the overgrown grass, sagging fence, and the dog shit just left, deposited by strays who had as little respect for their property as everyone else? Yet she was surprised by the boy's boldness in her mother's presence—his voice was much clearer and more direct speaking now to Mary than when he'd spoken to her. Usually, her mother had the opposite effect on people. They'd look away, or stare for just a moment too long while finding the words to speak to her. Grace knew that she possessed no such mesmeric beauty.

Mary considered his request for a moment. Grace could almost count the myriad concerns scuttling across her mother's mind. Then, despite herself, Mary gave a cheerful answer.

"Okay. Yes. Pull out those weeds in the front over there. Just don't tramp on my plants. And when you're done with that, sweep the back stoep. The yard broom is behind the house."

He nodded. "Okay, Auntie."

For a moment, Grace expected a smile, but his features remained somber.

"And Johnny," Mary added haughtily.

"Yes, Auntie?'

"I am not your auntie. Mrs. de Leeuw will do."

Grace found her mother's boldness uncharacteristic. Her excitement about having the boy in their yard was tempered by a fear of what could happen when Patrick returned home. For Mary to even have spoken to the boy came as a surprise. She knew her mother thought of the people next door as low class, not worthy of association. Shortly after Johnny's arrival, Grace had heard her complain to Patrick.

"It's not enough for them to breed like rats anymore. Now they have to take in other people's throwaways? Where did the boy come from? What has he already seen in life? He has a dark look about him, that one. He'll be a bad influence on the others."

Patrick had ignored her.

Grace watched Johnny sweep the back yard, careful not to disturb the delicate fall of the lace curtain lest he notice her interest. When Mary found her at her vantage point she snapped at her.

"What do you think you're doing? Come away from that window. What if he sees you? What will he think?"

Grace wandered off to her bedroom. With her homework done, there was nothing to do except listen to the radio. She turned up the volume of Springbok Radio's request hour just enough so that the sound filled her room without drifting through the rest of the house, and along with George Michael, lamented the careless whispers of good friends. Mary hated loud music blaring from the house—it gave a bad impression, she said.

Later on her way to the living room, Grace passed the kitchen, where she found her mother, to the left of the window, transfixed, as she watched Johnny work. Grace glided by, not daring to disturb whatever was happening in Mary's mind.

By the time Patrick returned from work, Johnny was already back next door. He didn't notice the neater yard, so Mary waited until suppertime until she broached the subject.

"Patrick," she started out in a confident tone, "that boy next door, you know, the new one, Johnny, came to knock here this afternoon. Asked if we had any work for him. I liked that, you know, trying to better himself. Trying to work. So I made him clean the yard, gave him fifty cents. He did quite a good job... surprisingly."

Across the blue kitchen table, Patrick stared at his wife. Grace held her breath. In those few brief sentences lay a world of potential hurt, a number of triggers to a range of explosions. He could be mad that she'd employed someone, spending his money, without asking. The mask of suspicion could settle over his face and he could accuse her of something with the boy. He could twist her words about trying to get a job into a slight, directed at his last six-month stint of unemployment, now thankfully over. He could take it as a dig at him for not doing the man's work of cleaning the yard. Grace looked down into her chicken curry, her appetite gone. She scraped bits of meat around in the rich, fragrant sauce, praying for this cup to pass.

When they came Patrick's words were low, filled with a building malice.

"I thought he was dirty, one of the rats. Not to be trusted."

Mary wilted. She had contradicted herself, and Patrick was seizing the gap between her stated stance and her actions today. More grievously, she had made a decision concerning the house and their lives without consulting him. Grace started silently to curse her mother. She should really know better by now than to do such things.

"Well, I thought it would be good, Patrick...."

"You thought, Mary?"

A crooked sneer contorted his face. Mary stiffened and placed her fork on her plate. His words were a direct challenge, a test of his dominion which she would have to pass in order for any of them to have the long, looming night be a peaceful one. Grace's silent prayers turned into a chant. Let it go, Mama, just let it go.

"I'm sorry, Patrick. I should have waited for you. I just thought, better than being idle....The devil finds work...." Her voice trailed off.

Grace fixated on her plate, sliding rice onto her fork without making any scraping noises. She had gotten a hiding for that before. Relief washed over her. Thank God Mary was making an effort to sound contrite.

"I'm really sorry, Patrick...." Her voice was tinged with desperation.

It struck the right note. Patrick sighed, nodded knowingly, and continued to eat his curry. The rest of the meal passed in silence.

After Grace cleared the supper dishes, Patrick went outside the back door to inspect Johnny's handiwork. He stayed out there for a long time, and when he returned, he leaned over the bottom half of the split back door, sun-kissed and smiling.

"The boy did a good job, Mary. We should let him come again."

Mary turned from the sink, smiled, and nodded. She had won his approval, had done something good. And there he was, smiling at her now, the light of love in his eyes reserved just for her. She had done something right and he'd seen it, acknowledged it. Mary blushed. Grace rolled her eyes. Her mother was too easy sometimes. Leaning across the door with a cigarette dangling from his lips, Patrick bantered and flirted with Mary as she and her mother finished the dishes. Buoyed by his mood, mother and daughter relaxed. The walls around them expanded a little, the house let out a sigh; the evening became lighter, and soon jokes were flying while Patrick, glowing, made the embers of the dying sun linger for a touch longer than usual. He called them his girls. This was the father Grace loved, the husband Mary adored. This Patrick was why she could not leave.

As he leaned over the bottom half of the door, it struck Grace again how handsome her father was when he smiled like this, how much she loved looking at the dark, smooth skin, the even features, and the strong jaw sprouting day-old stubble. He came inside, strode over to Mary, and scooped her into a firm embrace as she giggled coyly. On evenings like that, when the tensions between them ebbed away, life tasted sweet like the overripe peaches hanging from the tree in their back yard.

Johnny worked his way into the De Leeuws' lives, quickly becoming a fixture. At first he appeared once a week with his bare, cracked feet and downcast look, waiting patiently for Mary to issue instructions. Then he'd set to work, methodically making his way through the back yard, pruning, weeding, and watering in silent concentration. He never asked for anything. He was content to do his work, shuffle to their back door when it was done and, always keeping his eyes to the floor, stretch out his palms to receive his fifty cents. So much like a beggar, Mary had mused aloud. She wondered if Johnny felt her mother's disdain. As the weeks gave way to months, his visits to their house became more frequent. Grace watched her mother soften toward the boy.

"He's not like all the others next door," Grace overheard her saying down the line to Aunty Joan. "His clothes are always clean; his mouth too. He doesn't swear or talk back, and he knows his place. Works hard."

This tenderness bemused Grace. It wasn't done for people

like hers, the De Leeuws, to mix with people like them: country bumpkins, coloureds from the farms who didn't speak English, who didn't even own shoes. Mary had always prided herself on the shoes they all owned and maintained, despite the scarcity of money. You judge a man by his shoes, she was fond of saying. But Johnny loosened something in her, and Grace watched with amazement as Mary's rigid rules about who was fit company for whom relaxed. On days when she arrived home early enough, she made the boy sandwiches while cooking supper. For Mary, this was a generous gesture, bold even. Although he was only a boy of thirteen, it still wasn't appropriate for him to come inside the house, so it fell to Grace to serve her mother's culinary gifts to Johnny in the back yard.

At first he'd say thank you and leave the food untouched until Grace went back inside, but as weeks passed, Grace began to linger in silence, sitting somewhere close to him but never making eye contact, tracing figures in the sand under some tree, or reacquainting soft fingers with steely blades of grass. At first Johnny ignored her, but one day, overcome with hunger, he could no longer play the game. He picked up the plate of sandwiches, moved under the shade of the apple tree, and crouched down on his haunches as he bit into the cheese and tomato snack. Grace watched him slyly. He closed his eyes for a few brief seconds after the first bite, then slowly devoured the food in giant bites, not once pausing to look up or around. Nothing else existed in the few seconds it took Johnny to eat the sandwich. When he was done, not a crumb was left. He got up and offered Grace the empty plate with a muted thank you. Grace stayed outside longer and longer on these errands to take Johnny his late lunch. Careful not to interrupt his culinary reverie—his pleasure in food seemed almost holy—Grace waited and waited until one day she was brave enough to ask him a question. Did he like school? His answer was curt, but once the ice had been broken their chats lengthened, becoming a ritual to which they both looked forward. By now, Johnny was doing yard work three times a week; for Grace, they were the best days of the week.

Patrick took a shine to Johnny too. He got into the habit of stopping to chat with the boy when he arrived home from work, demonstrating this technique for pruning a bush or that way of softening a hard patch of earth. Some nights he lingered for up to half an hour before stepping inside to take off his work overalls, smoking one cigarette after the other as he talked to the boy. On these nights, Grace brooded behind the lace curtains, watching with an odd mix of repulsion and delight, as the man and boy unfolded toward each other. They were similar in stature. Both were muscular, but where Patrick was compact, Johnny had a leanness that belied his physical strength. At thirteen, Johnny was nudging past Patrick in height. Both had deep brown skin, polished to a high gloss. Johnny's manner remained deferential; most often his eyes stayed on the ground as a sign of respect to the older man. In turn, Patrick's stiff, pent-up manner relaxed with each encounter. Each time they spoke, he moved a little closer, gestured a bit larger, stayed outside a bit later with Johnny. From her spot behind the lace curtain Grace watched them, thrilled at first by their closeness and witnessing the firm affection she'd develop for Johnny transfer to her father.

Until Johnny, Grace and Patrick had had few things in common. She stayed out of his way, speaking only when spoken to, waiting for him to talk to her, ask her about school, her friends. When she was younger he'd tell her stories—wonderful, phantasmagorical tales of animals who talked and commandeered their own ships out at sea; his swims as a young man out to Seal Island; his encounters with great white sharks. There were walks in the green swathe of land between the airport and their house where they picked flowers, examined chameleons, pulled out long reeds and sucked on their sweet, white ends. But as she grew older, Grace could not hold her father's attention. Whatever demons lived in him started turning on her too, with increasing venom, and she slipped from his affection and he from hers. She could tell when he was drunk, at first by smelling his breath, later on by mere sight of the eerie, veiled glow that enlivened his eyes when he'd had too much. She had come to anticipate the inevitable violence that would follow most bouts of drinking. She learned to steer clear, become invisible. In that state, the very sight of her could set Patrick off.

"You!" he would scream. "Why you? Why not my son?"

This rant, unfathomable to Grace, was often the trigger to violence. Grace was an occasional target for beatings, but the full might of his blows were reserved for Mary. Grace never witnessed them. Even in supreme states of drunkenness, Patrick made sure that no one saw, not even Grace, who followed Mary around like a puppy, and who found the bouts of violence all the more terrifying for hearing but not being able to see them.

The sounds of her father's fists landing on Mary paralyzed Grace, while Mary's screams were an agony ripping through her chest. What was he doing to her? Where was he hitting? She heard every note of this warped symphony play out in grotesque detail. First Mary's plea—"Please no, please don't"—his voice raised, his fist striking flesh. A fresh cry from Mary, another and yet another blow. Violent, electrifying. Charging the air. A thud. Her head against the cupboard, or his body against the door? A crash. Perhaps a table falling or a chair hitting the floor after imprinting itself onto Mary's body? Silence. Then a series of pathetic sobs, the sound of a soul breaking, and after that a fading into nothingness. Snoring. Her mother venturing to move, creeping out of the room. Water running in the bathroom. Mary's footsteps at Grace's bedroom door; her body slipping gingerly in beside Grace's rigid one. Grace regulating her breathing, pretending to be asleep, pretending not to have heard.

On nights Patrick wasn't home, Mary drew the night around them like a soft, velvet cloak. Huddled together under the covers of her queen-size bed, she plucked stars out of the sky and spread them before Grace in a glittering private feast: the daintiest chocolate squares squirreled away for such occasions; candied oranges dipped in chocolate; toast triangles, crusts removed, topped with slivered avocado; sweet, milky tea in fine china cups, warmed milk frothing against dainty rims. Decadent treats, hidden from him during the days and nights he was present, brought out on lace-covered trays on nights he forgot about Grace and Mary and found the lure of drink and women stronger than the need to be home. It was part of the warped economy of the house. They could not afford to paint the outside, but locked away inside was the best china Mary's money could buy. No one had money to fix the sagging gutters or broken bathroom window, which was papered over with plastic, and yet on Friday when she got her pay packet, Mary brought home tinned oysters and fine chocolate. On nights she laid out these feasts they gorged on treats while Mary threw her own personal handfuls of stars—her stories—back into the breathless sky. There was something about the dark intimacy of night, the drawing of curtains and the warmth of a bedside light that made Mary come alive. Her voice became low and seductive, her eyes sparkled, her pinned hair came cascading down her shoulders, free, as she regaled Grace with tales of her childhood.

"Did I tell you about that time, I was about your age...?"

"No, Mama, you didn't," Grace would lie. "Tell me now."

"Well, I had already discovered boys. I wasn't shy like you. Now one boy in particular had his eye on my friend, or so we thought. But all the time, it was really me he was after. And one day, there he was, standing outside our door early one morning, waiting for me with a bunch of flowers in his hands, picked from the neighbors' gardens. Can you imagine the sight? Lovelorn, he was, completely silly-eyed!" The pleasure of recollection brought a smile to her face. She smiled coquettishly, as if flirting with Grace.

Stories like these made Grace feel inadequate, like a colorless, watered down copy of her mother. Suitors were not exactly lining up outside their door for her. There were other stories, too, not of Mary's legendary beauty or the folly it inspired. These were about the priceless trove of oil paints that had been bequeathed to Mary by the white madam of a neighbor, how each fat tube had contained an entire universe of color. Mary had sat with them for hours at first, just taking them in, getting to know them. Then she had worked up the nerve to shoplift a set of brushes at an art supply shop in the city and scavenged some leftover rolls of paper outside a paper warehouse. All by herself, she had learned the properties of the oils applied in different strokes, with different sized brushes, and had moved on to mixing them to form new colors. With her paints and brushes Mary had created entire worlds, private worlds of delight born out of nothing but her imagination.

"What happened to your paintings?" Grace asked one night.

"He threw them out, my father. Told me to stop wasting time with such silly nonsense."

"But why?"

"He wanted me to learn something useful, something that

would make a good job until I found a husband."

They'd giggle at the mention of said husband. Things hadn't worked out the way Mary's father had planned.

"Why don't we do that now? Paint?" Grace tried.

And Mary would exhale the wordless sigh of a woman who had surrendered her dreams to the world too soon.

On Patrick's absent nights, Mary's stories could entertain Grace for only so long. On these nights, there would come the inevitable hour when silence dropped over the house, and they pricked their ears for his footstep long before his key turned in the front door lock. When stories dried up and treats were gobbled, Grace would be dispatched to bed, lights out. Mary would wait in the bedroom, not yet asleep, since that, too, could trigger his fury no matter how neat the house or how warm the supper.

Sometimes their preemptive measures were enough, and he would fall asleep after wolfing down some food. At other times, seeking an outlet for his rage, Patrick would stumble into Grace's room, wake her on the pretext of her not having completed this or that chore, and scold her: for being lazy, for being careless, for being awake, for being alive, for daring to live when his precious firstborn son could not. As if her coming was something she had planned, as if it had taken up the very air her dead brother was meant to breathe. On those nights, Grace was the valve Patrick needed to let off the bitter steam of grief and rage. And once he had awoken his fury, he would take it into the next room and vent it upon Mary.

He apologized the next day, every time, blaming his violence on drink. But sober, too, he could be violent, though in a much more controlled way. Grace learned to stay out of his way then as well, perfecting the calculus of being present in a room without having that presence felt, of speaking without being heard, of living without interrupting the threadbare cloak of respectability Mary stitched out of nothing to hang around her family. Father and daughter became strangers. Grace stayed out of his way; hated him. And yet, she yearned for him and the love he had once shown and that still lingered in her memory. She longed for him to pick her up and embrace her, even though she was too big for all of that now. She wished for the times when he would hold her hand when they crossed a street. She longed for another extravagant story. She wanted him to lean into her when he spoke, the way she now saw him leaning in toward Johnny as she watched them through the window as the light faded.

Patrick rested his hand on Johnny's shoulder and something ripped inside of her. In that instant, she hated Johnny; wanted him to get away from her family and out of her life. Why had they ever let him in? They had been fine, just the three of them, even with their problems. At least her parents had been hers and hers only. Grace went to bed nursing horrible thoughts, hating both Johnny and her father, who seemed especially cheerful when he finally came inside that night.

She could never hold a grudge against Johnny for too long, though. The next time she saw him, he smiled as he held a peach out to her, the best one from the tree. His shy smile melted her, and soon she was laughing and teasing. Johnny pulled her braids, pretending to sweep her feet with the yard broom. They sat down under the plum tree, and looking at his open lovely face, still childish but revealing the features of the man he'd become, Grace forgave her father for loving Johnny. Who wouldn't love him, this Johnny? She realized then, with an unfamiliar tremble, that what she felt for him was love; that she thought of him as hers. Her Johnny, now gone.

It was well after midnight and people were still coming and going next door. Johnny must not be home yet. The smell of petrol clung to the air, and the night sky held an unnatural orange glow, which meant the fires the students had lit earlier in the day were still burning.

Grace was looking at the troubled sky when a figure took shape outside her bedroom window. Petrified, she froze, unable to scream. A man was creeping toward her. A soldier—coming to finish the work of today. One of those who were at the school and who had taken Johnny away, had teargassed them and shot everyone. Grace felt certain she was about to die, in her bed, the one place that was supposed to be safe. The figure grew larger as it came closer. A hand reached out. Grace found her voice and unleashed a siren-like, unearthly scream at the same time as the features of the shadow figure came into focus. It was her father.

Chapter 7

Patrick woke up with a throbbing head and a dark mood upon him. It hurt even to roll out of bed. He cursed himself silently for having drunk so much. As the night's events floated back into consciousness, he moved to cursing Mary instead. Damn bitch! All he had done was go to the house to see whether Grace was okay. He had just wanted to see her, hold her against him, feel her breathing; but Mary had been a bitch about it, as usual, and had denied him that. She must have known by then that the boy next door, Johnny, was missing. Surely she should have been able to imagine Patrick's distress at this news. What harm would it have done to let him in? To sit with Grace for a few minutes? It was the most horrible of times, police going mad, shooting children, and here Mary was, stubborn, defiant, denying him his duty to protect his family. Denying him the very thing that made him a man. He stood up, casting around for something to drink. In the little shack he now called home there was nothing. He did not even own a refrigerator—his meals, prepared on a single-burner gas stove, required few ingredients.

Patrick had been doing all right. Mary had kicked him out many times before. This time, too, he was sure he'd be allowed back after a suitable penance. He had been determined to stop drinking for good. And though this split between them had been the longest yet, he had not touched a drop since they'd parted. He had stayed with his new job, turning up each morning ten minutes before starting time. He was making a go of this new life. He had left the old drinking friends behind. Once he had even gone to Mass, but he found he could not stand being within the confines of a Catholic church—the incense choked him and every time he went down on his knees he had the dizzying sensation of some big unseen hand trying to topple him. He left before the service was over, bathed in cold sweat, as if some ungodly force had wanted him gone. He found some solace at the big tent —less morose, no incense to choke him; all in all, a much more pleasant place. He'd even been baptized again, and the goodwill he'd received afterwards had helped him keep it together. He had been doing all right—until last night.

Sick with worry about Johnny and infuriated by Mary's callous words, he had had nowhere to turn. He had wanted to help look for the boy, but when he went to Tim and Rowena's it was obvious he was not needed. He had wanted to sit with Grace, but was not wanted there either. He had needed the girl, perhaps more than she'd needed him, he now admitted to himself. He needed the coltish limbs, the just-washed child smell of her hair, the thin brown arms around his neck. He imagined picking her up like he used to do when she was a small child, when she'd wait for him at the end of the long passage and would charge at him the moment he'd step inside the door. He'd scoop her up, she'd throw her arms around him, and they would dance, she squealing with delight. Of course she was too grown up for all of that now, but last night Patrick had needed to feel that old connection between them. He admitted for the first time, as the feeling of impotence had subsided after Mary had turned him away, that he missed her.

Patrick wondered again how Grace had gone from gurgling toddler, to laughing child who clung to his every word, to surly young girl. It was as if one moment she was there smiling up at him, and the next she had turned into a diminutive replica of Mary, eyes filled with recrimination whenever she looked at him. He knew he had not been the perfect husband and father—that the reality of his life fell far short from the vision he had had for himself on the day he had married Mary. He knew he could be cruel. He was ashamed, always, in his sober moments, of the way he had turned to violence. He knew it was a weakness, an addiction, like the addiction to drink. He felt contempt for himself with each failure to give it up, and then, sensing their contempt, turned his self-hatred outward, demanding respect. It had been a big disappointment to overcome when Grace was born, that she was a girl, especially after his first loss. But Patrick felt he had made a decent attempt, although he was bitter at first, to be a good father to her. Grace was quiet in nature, not at all a demanding infant, and he had found himself softening toward her even as he further hardened himself against Mary after the birth. He had desperately wanted a son and held Mary somehow accountable for this hole in his life. With Grace's birth, the hole had become even bigger. But by the time she was two, Patrick could say that he loved her; loved the little thing who had crept into his heart.

He did not believe in loving too much, in showing too much weakness or indulging a child in a way that made him think she was the center of the world. Patrick had no time for that. Children should know their place. Patrick parented according to a series of unwritten rules: the child should not approach or speak to him first; she should never talk back when reprimanded; she should have a healthy level of responsibility. There should be a healthy distance between parent and child, especially father and child. Yet when he could bring himself to enter into Grace's world, on her terms, Patrick was enchanted by her attention to the tiniest detail, her questions, her sense of wonder at the world and the way it worked. He took her on expeditions into the bush, watched, a little awestruck, as she discovered this bug, or that flower, and lost herself in it. There was an innocence about her that disarmed him, and yet it also stirred up resentment in him, for was this state of grace not what he had known and lost, had spent the rest of his life trying to retrieve? He had known it at some point, but had unremembered it. It had not been protected and nurtured in him, and now it was lost. He hated his parents and the others who had forced it out of him when he thought about life in this way, and then, momentarily, hated the girl for her unencumbered state of being.

It was in such moments that he would say something ugly, do something destructive, like squash the bug she'd been looking at. It was as if Patrick, in a state of half-jealousy, half-protectiveness, wanted to squash the innocence right out of her; as if by such an act, he could say in action what he could not articulate: who do you think you are, to have awe and wonder of this world? Do you not know who you are? Do you not know your place in this world, this country? Do you not know that dreaming is dangerous, and not for your kind?

Whenever he had such an outburst, the child would react strangely. Grace would not cry or ask why he had inflicted a cruelty upon her. Instead, she would lift her eyes at him in hurt bemusement, never daring an utterance. As she grew up, that look came more and more frequently, sometimes overlaid with resignation, at other times with disgust, until one day, Patrick could not stand to look at her. He could feel the reproach in her gaze. Shame was replaced with resentment. He would think about his son, his perfect son, the one who would have looked like him and worshipped him, and he thought of the unfairness of it all, of how he was stuck instead with this creature and her accusatory eyes. Those eyes—wanting, wanting, always wanting something from him that he could not give. His feelings for Grace became a convoluted knot of love and resentment.

Last night he had needed that loving little girl, and Mary had denied him. Half-mad, he had fallen back into old ways: frightened for Johnny, and missing his girl, he had gone back to the shebeen from which he'd exiled himself for six months. There he received a rousing welcome, and soon, with a whiskey melting the tension in his stomach, he wondered why he had ever stayed away. Just one, maybe two; he could handle it this time. He had not had a drink in six months and could now stop at any time. A pleasant, numbing warmth spread through his body. His shoulders softened, face relaxed. Grace was okay, the boy from next door would be found, he would get back together with Mary again. The second drink was easier to take; the third even easier. It was after midnight when he left the shebeen. He started down to his new place, then changed his mind and direction. Fuck it, he thought. She was not going to keep him away from his daughter.

The house was swaddled in darkness. Even drunk, Patrick knew his approach should best not happen from the front door. There was no way Mary would open it for him, not after last night's showdown. He thought about Grace, tucked up in bed. He would go to her window, say goodnight, give her a kiss through the bars; conspire against Mary as they used to when Grace was still little.

In his mind's eye, Grace would be happy to see him. She would giggle a little and hold his hand, because surely she had missed him too? Instead, her screams startled him. Then Mary started screaming too. Lights went on inside the house and next door. "It's me; it's only me!" He'd shouted through the closed window.

But by then the pair were hysterical and could not hear him. Tim, along with a convoy of men armed with batons, rushed over.

"What is going on here! What are you doing, man?"

"It's me, Patrick! I live here. Fuck you! Can a man not see his own family?"

That goddamn Mary. This was what she had reduced him to— a simpering coward, begging for them to recognize him. Worked up as they were about Johnny, it would take nothing for one of these men to plant a pole against his skull. Bitch! How could she do this to him!

"Sorry, man. But why you crawling around like a thief?"

"Can a man not see his own family!" he shouted again, bolstered in his righteous fury by the recognition that he was safe, that at least these men would not harm him. "I just want to see my family!" This time the words were accompanied by a wild, swinging fist, which shattered the girl's bedroom window.

"Come, come now, Patrick. It's hard, but you know you have to go." Tim was soothing in his tone, trying to dispel any looming violence. He had seen before what Patrick was capable of.

"Come, Patrick, come. It's time to go home. We'll walk a way with you."

"Fuck you! I don't need you to tell me when to come and go in my own fucking yard!"

Nevertheless, far outnumbered and surrounded by men, Patrick allowed himself to be led away from the window and onto the gravel road. The men formed a laager around him and moved him down Saturn Street—his street, on which he no longer lived.

Patrick did not remember how he'd gotten back to the little room he now called home. His head hurt. He picked up an empty enamel pot from the floor, went outside and filled it with water from a tap attached to the main house. He lit the gas ring and put the water on for coffee, then fingered the gash on the fist that had broken the window. It was far too late to go to work, and since it was almost noon, he would be docked half the day's wages anyhow. It didn't make sense for him to go, not the way his head was pounding, and with a useless hand. He summoned the night before into his thoughts. What the hell was wrong with Grace? How could his own child not recognize him? Did she do that to antagonize him, make him more of the bad guy than he already was? He hated that the neighbors had witnessed it all. After the last episode, the one that made Mary decide to finally end it, they had looked at him differently. He could feel their contempt in their stiffened spines when he passed them, even the men. He had only wanted to see his daughter, and then, this scene.

Patrick needed to redeem himself. To do this, he would have to take his place again as head of his household. He knew that last night's behavior was unacceptable, but if he could talk to Mary one more time, just one more, he was sure he would make her see that his frustration was a measure of his desperation to be back with them. I did this because I love you, he would say to Mary. It was true, and she needed to hear it. Patrick fixed upon a plan to go and see her again, a plan to make her see reason. She wouldn't be home for a few hours, which gave him time to have just one drink. Yes, a drink would calm him and give him the courage he needed to convince Mary. He would have just one; he knew he could do it, and by the time she got home it would have worn off anyway. She wouldn't even notice. And so, at noon, Patrick headed back to the shebeen for one last drink.

Chapter 8

Mary entered the bedroom where her daughter lay in bed. She put a steaming cup of tea on the bench beside her.

"Morning, Grace!"

She was already dressed for work, her face sharp and fresh from the colors painted there, but not even her most expensive potion could mask the circles under her eyes. The false cheer grated on Grace.

"Is Johnny back?"

"No, my baby. I've heard nothing."

She lit a cigarette and inhaled deeply. No words were spoken about what had happened the night before—that was not Mary's way. Mary had been frantic in her rush to get into the bedroom after Grace's screams and the breaking window woke her. Protective like a lioness, she'd grabbed Grace out of bed in one furious swoop and had locked them both in the main bedroom, shoving an ineffectual chair against the door for good measure. That was a well-worn routine: on nights before when Patrick's seething threatened quick fruition, they often locked themselves in the nearest room that had held onto its door. Some nights he would leave them alone and go to sleep; some nights he broke through the cheap chipboard with one or two jabs of his fists. As a result, the doors in the house on Saturn Street had a lot of holes in them, which Mary patched up with pretty floral wallpaper that she kept for this purpose. But if a door was assaulted one time too many, it became useless and had to be removed. You could only patch a holey door so many times with wallpaper. If a bedroom door was removed, Patrick would transfer an unscathed door from a less private part of the house to the bedroom—there was never money to buy new doors. By the time he left, Mary and Grace had just about run out of functional doors. And though he wasn't even in the house the night before, Mary's old instinct had kicked in, and before they knew what was happening, she was locked safely with Grace behind her bedroom door. There they remained, silent, breathless, listening hard to the comforting voices of men from next door trying to coax Patrick away from the house.

When they were sure Patrick was gone from outside Grace's bedroom, they ventured back in there to survey the damage. Glass shards littered Grace's bed. Mary gave the bedding a quick tug, shaking bits of glass down the back of the bed.

"Just don't put your hand down," she warned Grace, while sweeping up the remaining shards into the middle of the room with a hand broom. Next Mary examined the damage to the window. The southeaster was strong, threatening to rip the remaining splintered edges out of the frame. That was the last thing they needed. Mary went to fetch her roll of wallpaper and her pot of wallpaper glue. She cut off a suitably sized rectangle and went to work.

"Just until we can fix it properly, okay?"

Grace glared at her, anger leeching through her eyes. Yes, of course. They'd fix it later, just like the rest of this broken down place would be magically fixed.

"Get back into bed now, Grace."

"But the glass!"

"It's okay. I took it all away."

Her mother could be so stupid sometimes, Grace thought, as she crept into the bed, which felt defiled. Why couldn't she just let her sleep next to her in the big bed?

When Grace woke, the morning sun revealed a blacked-out window—a rotten tooth in an otherwise glistening smile. Fresh rage built in Grace as she wiped the sleep out of her eyes. Revulsion churned inside her: for the house, her father, even Mary; the ugliness of it all. And there was Mary now, with her tea and her stinking cigarettes, pretending that nothing had happened. Grace felt like hitting her.

"Now listen, Grace, I want you to pay attention to what I'm going to say."

Another match struck the tinder against the Lion box; another cigarette glowed to life as Mary sucked on it, eyes closed with pleasure. "Yes, Mama."

"I have to go to work today. I wish I could stay but I can't. Don't go to school. You hear me? Don't. I don't want you to set a foot outside of this house today. Understand?"

Grace nodded. She used to love school. It was the one place where she understood the rules, where, if she followed them, results were consistent and predictable. That was before the damned State of Emergency.

"Stay away from the windows. If you hear shooting, any noise, I want you to drop on the floor, no matter where you are. Stay away from the windows, you hear? Don't open the door for anyone: not your friends, not the neighbors, not Johnny, not police. And especially not for your father. Do you understand me, Grace?" The gold cross bobbed up and down at Mary's throat as she became more adamant, more animated, in her instructions to Grace.

"Yes, Mama," Grace assented, while inside her a voice screamed, Bitch! What kind of woman leaves her child when there are evil men roaming around, lurking outside the windows, shooting? Her father was right about Mary: heartless. Mary leaned forward to kiss her, but Grace pulled away.

Mary, with wounded eyes, turned and left for work without another word. Smoke trailed in her wake. Grace heard the grind of her key in the security gate, and then there was silence.

"Bye, Mama!" she shouted, too late. Mary was already gone.

Now it was just Grace, alone in ugly old number twenty-one, which now had another scar, as it sighed under the assault of the southeaster. Grace hated the place: the walls weeping pieces of paint like oversized dandruff flakes; the cobwebs merrily suspended from the ceiling like forgotten Christmas decorations; the curtains, faded and encrusted with dust and dried coffee from the time when Patrick threw a full cup at Mary.

She got up reluctantly and wandered into her parents' bedroom, finding it in a state of complete disarray. The bed was unmade and Mary's clothes were piled high up on the threadbare armchair in the corner, their colors and textures in stark contrast to the drabness of the rest of the room. On Mary's nightstand an overflowing ashtray stood on top of an Agatha Christie thriller. Her empty teacup had lost its matching saucer, etching yet another ring into the surface of the nightstand. Grace turned to face her mother's huge mahogany dresser with its winged, three-part mirror. She ran her fingers across the surface of the wood, gathering dust at their tips, and stared for a long time at her reflection. A pleasant round face, nut-brown skin, and adequately pretty eyes returned her gaze. An ordinary face—nothing to distinguish it from any other face you might see around here. Who would she become? More than anything, Grace wanted to be a beauty, the kind of beauty her mother was, the kind that turned heads, eliciting widened eyes and deferential bows. She wanted the kind of beauty that left men begging outside your door for one last chance to see your face. She fumbled with a few tiny bottles on the dresser, then unscrewed one of them and poured a dab of its contents into her palm. Elegant Ivory concealer. She warmed the contents in the palm of one hand with the fingers of the other as she'd watched her mother do a million times and dabbed it on her face with series of light, swift pats. The concealer sat on top of her dark skin like chalk on a board, refusing to blend—she looked painted like a clown, not elegant like her mother, whose skin tone was a perfect match to the bottle's contents. Maybe some blush would settle it, she thought. With broad brushstrokes she painted on the peachy-pink, glittery powder her mother used. She followed it with a generous application of fuchsia lipstick. Maybe this would be the magic wand that transformed her into Mary.

Her work done, Grace stood back, looking at her reflection from all angles, and sighed. She might as well accept that she looked like him. Had her nose been a little less flat and her hair just a bit straighter, she would have been a pretty girl. Sometimes, when she stared long enough at herself in the mirror, she could see the transformation of sharper, sleeker features take place. She had Mary's eyes, which was a good start, but Grace's kroes hair and darker skin always made her feel like a cheap knock-off of her mother. Mary could have passed for white had she not married Patrick, Ouma loved to say.

Enough of this, Grace decided, whipping a tissue out of a box on the dresser with which to wipe the Elegant Ivory sludge from her face. Mary had bought it a few months ago after a particularly brutal fight. She couldn't stay away from work again with yet another blue eye, and heavy with guilt, Patrick had given her R10 to spend on whatever she needed to get her face fit for public. Grace was with her when she walked up to the makeup counter at Greatermans, where she waited, eyes down, for all the other women at the counter to be served first. "Well, somebody got a good hiding," the woman behind the counter sneered at Mary.

Never before had Grace seen her mother bow her head like that in public, not even around white people. Grace clung a little closer to her, tightening her grip on Mary's arm. The woman behind the shiny glass counter brought down a bottle of Elegant Ivory from a mirrored shelf, but refused to let Mary try a sample, as other women had been doing.

"You want it, you buy it. I can't have a coloured use the same sample I use for the other ladies."

Mary slid her R10 note across the counter, slipped the packaged bottle into her handbag and, head still bowed, left the department store without waiting for her change.

"Come!"

She had grabbed Grace's hand as they moved through the swishing doors that magically parted before them. Grace had never seen Mary cower to white people: her mother didn't care for them, didn't respect them, was indifferent to them outside of what she needed to do for them at work. But that day she had been shamed in front of them by Patrick's hand, her proud head bowed by his public humiliation. And there he was, waiting for them outside the fancy shop, eyes glistening with shame and puppy-dog love. He moved toward them and tried to slip an arm around Mary's shoulder. Grace fought the urge to kick his shins, scream at him to leave her mother the hell alone. She wanted to shout it in front of the whole world, in the middle of the milling Saturday morning shoppers, what a fuck-up he was, how she wished he would die. Mary had shrugged off Patrick's gesture. Good, Grace thought, as she shot him a smug little smile. She doesn't need you. People were staring at them as they moved this shame-inflected dance through the parking lot.

Grace removed the last traces of Elegant Ivory from her face and glanced at her mother's bedside clock—it was only nine. The day stretched before her like a nightmare. She had library books to read, but didn't feel like reading, and there was nothing else to do between these walls. Where was Johnny? Was he hurt, in pain? Had he even woken up this morning? She would go next door for a quick visit, despite Mary's warnings, and find out the latest. He might even be back.

The sun had come out from behind the clouds and was straining through the bedroom curtains. Grace wanted to go, but was scared of disobeying orders, even though Patrick was no longer around to enforce his particular brand of discipline. There was also the matter of the soldiers. It was hard to tell what was going on in their corner of the Cape Flats this morning: there could be rioting and shooting just a few blocks away, but because their house lay on the outskirts of the township, Grace wouldn't know that until the chaos spilled onto their street. Springbok Radio revealed nothing but Esmé Euvrard gurgling a cheerful request for an Aunty Liesbet. She would go, just for five minutes. What could happen in five short minutes?

Grace opened the front door, pausing for a moment before unlocking the security gate, the final barrier between the public and private. Save for the howl of the wind, everything was quiet. Fresh air rushed into the living room, forcing out the stale smell of cigarette smoke. She inhaled deeply. The air was good, so clean. Spring was here. Outside the southeaster was blowing madly, chasing wisps of streaky white cloud across a blue sky. It lifted her spirits. She stepped onto the path and headed next door to Johnny's place.

Grace had never before been inside the garage that housed Johnny and his family, even though it was only a few meters away from her back door. Rowena was sitting at an old wooden table, surrounded by women. Grace hesitated in the doorway, unnoticed, behind some women from around the neighborhood. One woman Grace didn't recognize had her arm around Rowena and was stroking her shoulders while making soft clucking noises. Rowena's face, red and swollen, told her all she needed to know —Johnny was not home.

"...all the hospitals, and the police stations...nothing."

The words drifted up at Grace, who was touched by the depth of Rowena's concern. Johnny was not her child, not even her own blood, but her distress was real, maternal. She had obviously not slept. Tim was going out of his mind, she heard Rowena say; she was worried he could snap at any moment and cause more trouble with the police.

From the door, Grace took in the details of Rowena, Tim, and Johnny's tiny home. The garage was divided into two rooms, separated by a row of dark cupboards. A wooden table anchored itself in the kitchen—clearly the hub around which this household revolved. Down a side wall stood a large green couch, now crammed with women whose bodies didn't quite hide its holes and the errant springs poking out underneath it. There was no kitchen sink, no taps for running water. A giant plastic tub stood on a bright orange cabinet—this was the sink in which they washed dishes, prepared food, and bathed. Next to it was a bucket used for fetching water from the outside tap that served all the tenants living in the neighbors' back yard. There was not much to see of the bedroom: a double bed covered with a velvety red bedspread peeked from behind the cupboards partitioning the space. For the first time, Grace wondered where Johnny slept. She could see no bed or space that would belong to him. She thought about her own room, the one she'd despised this very morning with its freshly broken window, and shame settled around her shoulders. At least she had a bed, warm blankets, could close the door when she wanted to be alone. At least she could imagine another time, another place, being grown up; in the privacy her room afforded she could imagine a different life. Shame dug in even deeper around her throat as she realized she had been close to Johnny for all these years, and now, for the first time, was taking in his home, without him there, without the women even noticing her. She felt like she was spying on Johnny's private world. It dawned on Grace why he spent so much time with them, even sitting in the kitchen having cups of tea with her parents on occasion; why she was never invited to his place. There really was no space that was his own, nowhere to sit and think, nowhere to dream.

More women arrived, their bodies pushing Grace inside the garage. Rowena started to sob quietly, and the weight of the bodies pressing against her became too much for Grace. She began to feel faint. Quietly, she worked her way back through the crush of bodies and out the door. She needed air, space.

And then she was running, as fast as her legs would carry her. She ran and ran, down Saturn Street, across an open field, past the last humble row of houses in the township, past the garbage dump that was always smoldering and belching its stench at them, across the busy arterial road leading to the winelands, and into the dense green bushes—uncluttered, uncultivated—the undeveloped, completely wild buffer zone left by developers to shield DF Malan Airport from the masses who lived just beyond it. From their back and front yards, Grace and others like her could see the planes take off like giant birds, hear their deafening roar when they came in to land, watch them glide and slice the sky on perfect, blue-sky Cape Town days. Only two miles away but, for most residents of the township, inaccessible as a dream forgotten upon waking. Why would they go there? What business could they possibly have at an airport, besides perhaps cleaning toilets or sweeping floors? Gravel crunching under her feet, hair flying, Grace knew she shouldn't be heading toward the dense bush that buffered the airport from her people, but the soft promise of green set off against a flawless blue sky, the knowledge of spring flowers turning their throats to the sun, the soft tranquility of the air, proved irresistible. They pulled at her feet and her heart.

She could already smell it, the air on that side of the road, infused with the scent of green leaves opening to sunlight, untouched by the smell of cooking, standing water, dog shit. She paused before dashing across the big road to the other side, the wild untrammeled place. Once she was across, where the road's black tar receded, small yellow flowers dotted the gravel and sand. They were a constellation of beaming suns lifting their heads in greeting toward her. Behind them stretched a lush expanse of green. Low, crouching clusters of shrubs, spilling leaves, and roots spreading like rivulets across the brown earth. Grass followed: green, red, and yellow grass, not clipped and disciplined like lawn but free, flowing and whispering in the wind. More yellow suns, and blue flowers too, swayed with the grass. Long grass brushed against her ankles. Grace stopped running and relaxed. She moved forward, deeper into the thicket, until her feet found the path that had been worn there by the two of them—she and Johnny. She moved onward until she felt the familiar dip in the sand and the leaves and branches suddenly danced against her chest. The bush enveloped her completely; the shrubs which seemed so small and lush from the other side of the road became a mess of sticks and prickly leaves. Grace walked on, through a tangle of gnarled and twisted branches until her head dipped beneath the canopy of leaves. Sunlight glinted, diamond like, through the roof of leaves above her. She went down on her hands and knees for some more space to move, and crawling, with sand granules filtering through her fingers like brown sugar, she entered into a new, magical world. Slowly, she made her way through the jungle, twisting and contorting her frame into whatever shape would allow her to negotiate the narrow gaps between the trunks. Her body found its rhythm against the thick foliage, and she moved, swayed along with it —a sigh in the breath of the bush as it whispered a prayer to the sun.

On the other side of the thicket, she stumbled out onto a grassy clearing. Here the grass was shorter and soft, inviting her to lie down and stretch, fully, in the sun. For the thousandth time, she marveled at this spot, this place that seemed to have been cleared especially for her, a space where she could just be. Wildflowers blossomed everywhere among the few low shrubs. Clumps of reeds dotted the periphery of the clearing, their brown fuzzy heads floating from pencil-thin stalks. A stately eucalyptus tree watched over it all, its branches throwing protective shade across her little patch of heaven. The clearing was anchored by a large rock, smooth at the base but jagged at the crown. This was Grace's personal throne; a couple of fat, lazy lizards her only companions. She touched her hand to the rock, relishing its texture, and flopped down beside it. Then she leaned her back against the smooth edge, arms stretched, legs out in front of her, with her bare toes splayed against the tree trunk. No one could see her, tell her to sit up straight or close her legs and act like a lady. Here Grace was in charge of her own queendom.

She was aware of the drone of distant traffic and then the sound of a plane coming in to land, thundering low across her spot. Once its noise receded into the distance, her ears picked out the hum of cicadas, the gentle swishing of reeds in the breeze. The first time she'd come here, years ago, she'd lost all concept of time, gotten home when the sun was dropping be-hind the mountain. Patrick had been pacing the front stoep like a caged animal, while her mother sighed in the living room with cigarette in hand. Where have you been? Worried sick! But not even a beating could force her to give up this place.

Today it was the perfect escape from the clucking, sympathetic tongues around Rowena, the stench of burning tires, broken windows, and the sounds of guns. Johnny might even appear: this had become their special place. About a year after he had started coming to their house she brought him here. She had never shown it to anyone before then, and in his quiet way Johnny belonged here too.

He was not like other boys who recklessly pitted themselves against nature, climbing and conquering trees or throwing stones at lizards. He had a respect for nature that mirrored hers. They'd spent hours at this very rock, laughing, talking, or just sitting together in silence. It was here that Johnny leaned over one day as they lay in the grass together and planted a gentle kiss on her lips.

"Why did you do that?" Grace had blurted out.

He'd looked down at the ground then, the way he used when they were still shy around each other. Embarrassment crept across her cheeks; embarrassment for herself, for reacting in such a childish, uncool way, coupled with a compounding shyness on his behalf, for his obvious, squirming discomfort.

"Well, you're a girl, I'm a boy," he'd said, as if that was all it really took for one person to start kissing another in the middle of nowhere. "And...I like you." His eyebrows rose into a question mark.

Grace had felt the heat rush to her face, and in her chest strange sensations bubbled, as if she hadn't eaten for days and had suddenly realized she was ravenous. The hunger spread across her chest. Johnny liked her? Not in the friend or family way, but like that, like a man liked a woman? No one had ever told her that they liked her; she had never even thought it possible, that in a universe of bold, outspoken, pretty girls with straight hair and wide hips, a boy could possibly be interested in her. When Grace dreamed about the future—when she was able to see a future— she was grown up with a husband who loved and took care of her. But in her imaginings the man who loved her always appeared in adulthood, after she had grown up and out of this unlovable skin; after she had shrugged off Patrick and the ugly house; after she had reinvented herself as a beautiful successful woman who looked like Mary; after she had cast off this ugly shell that was only temporarily Grace, and the ugly things that had happened to her. Her life would begin after she grew up. This here, now, was not really her life. It was just a period of waiting—waiting for her father to leave or die, for Mandela to come out of prison, for her mother to be happy and free. This was not anything really, this waiting. When it was over, that was when her life would really start. Then. Then there would be men who loved, when she could step away from this and love herself. She blushed in dazed awe that anyone could find something loveable in her and knew, immediately, that she loved Johnny back. She would always love him. She knew this on the day he kissed her. Her Johnny.

A plane took off, its orange tailfin glistening in the sun. Grace looked up, tracking its journey across the sky and prayed, harder than she'd ever prayed before: bring him back! She begged God, the plane, the trees, the grass, the distant mountain, the infinite blue sky—which, stretching as it did around the world, surely must see him. Bring him back! She got onto her knees beside the rock and prayed, until prayer rose up from every molecule in her body, until she became the very breath of God, until she was nothing but spirit, soaring up to the heavens, whispering in His ear: bring Johnny back!

When she was done, the sun hung low in the sky, ready to dip behind the unmoved face of Table Mountain. Calm settled over her. Leaves glowed in this magical light, knitting into Grace's bones the quiet surety that Johnny was alive and would be found. He would be found and would come back, and everything would go back to how it was before—no, better than before, with her father at a safe, bearable distance.

She got up from the clearing and pushed her way back through the branches and bushes to the tarred road that divided the bushy expanse from the township. It had grown late and people were coming back from work. Streams of cars were winding their way home on the old, too narrow arterial road. She waited too long, losing her nerve several times, before dodging between cars and getting halfway. Then she spent too long hopping about in the middle of the road on the white line where she shouldn't have been. Finally, safely on the other side, things were quiet. There was no sign of the armored vultures. Outside Johnny's home, people were still milling about, some with bowls of food covered in dishcloths. She could see Tim waving his arms, his gesticulation stirring a group of men into action. It looked like they were ready to depart on another search. Johnny was still not home.

Grace had just reached her house and was about to walk through the low front gate when on the corner a familiar figure came into view. The swagger in his gait revealed what Grace instinctively felt—that he'd had a few drinks—no, more than a few. There are times when a body knows, just knows, before the brain catches up, that it's in mortal danger. For Grace, that time was now. Heart pounding, she ran up to the security gate, and with fingers turning numb, fumbled to unlock it. A few quick prods at the lock, and the key took on a leaden weight of its own and gave up the fight against gravity. Dropped. She turned, and he was there, behind her, upon her, his body blocking out the sun and Grace from any passerby's view.

"Hello, Grace! How's my girl?"

Smiling. Drunk. Eyes aglow with a brewing storm. "Daddy...." She nodded.

"Where have you been, Gracie?"

"Nowhere...."

"Whoring around like your mother?"

Grace stopped struggling with the key, defeated. She wanted to hit him in his belly and see him cry with pain, but there she was, trapped between him and the security door with no chance to inflict an equivalent wound on him, no chance to get away.

"Pick up the key."

His voice was low, almost a whisper, chilling to her ear.

Grace obeyed the command. "Now unlock the door."

The dutiful daughter obeyed. Mama's words—"Whatever you do, don't let him in!"—screamed through her mind as the rest of her body went numb. From the corner of her eye she saw a convoy of cars, led by Tim's yellow Mazda, pass by. All the men from next door were gone.

The gate swung open. Impatiently, Patrick grabbed the keys from her and unlocked the front door. She was never quick enough. His hand closed like a vice on her upper arm, and in one powerful, practiced movement, he launched her unresisting body across the threshold and into the dark living room with its curtains all drawn. Grace picked herself up from her landing spot on the floor and sank into the dirty white couch, tightly wrapping her arms around her body. She kept her eyes on the floor, taking in the minutiae of today's sand arrangement on the carpet. No matter how she tried to clean it (Mary had long ago given up), the sand had a way of creeping back into the house, reclaiming its lost kingdom. Steel-toed work boots came and went across the still life of the floor, carrying the upturned cuffs of dark blue jeans, resting neatly above laced shoe tongues. Grace focused hard on the brown laces, moving slowly in and out of focus, in and out of her tableau of carpet and uncontrollable sand.

She heard the click of the front door being locked. The boots finally came to rest right in front of her, toe-to-toe with her own takkied feet.

"Look at me!"

She knew she had to, but she couldn't. Her shoulders were two blocks of ice, solid, pressing the rest of her body down into the couch.

"I said, look at me!"

A blow landed on Grace's left cheek, forcing movement from her stubborn head. She tried to hold back prickly tears, but they rolled down her cheeks as she tilted her head upwards, slid off her chin, and plopped onto the tops of her hands. Anger, pain, and shame coloured the contours of her face.

"Okay! I'm looking at you now! Happy?" The voice came from some unknown place, someone she didn't know. Her mouth was moving, contorting furiously, but it wasn't Grace screaming, it wasn't her voice escaping at a feverish pitch. "Are you happy now? Bastard!"

Grace wanted this voice to stop, knowing that it put her in grave danger, but she couldn't will it back into silence. It snaked from her throat, lashing him, cursing him. Spitting upon him.

"Fuck you, bastard! Pig! You destroy everything!"

Another open hand slap against her face. Tears, snot, and saliva gushed from her until she felt her head grabbed and her words smothered by his strong hands. Grace screamed, a sound swallowed by his callused palm. She tried to bite the inside of Patrick's hand, but he only clenched tighter, until all breath escaped her.

"Shush, shush, Grace." His voice dropped to a mere whisper. "Quiet, girl."

Gradually, her convulsive sobs subsided. There was a strange look in his eyes as her body slackened under his grip. It was as if he saw her for the first time, the real Grace. He released her and sat down on a chair across from the couch.

"Be quiet, okay?"

They contemplated each other, each summing the other up.

It struck Patrick for the first time: his daughter was growing up. Her limbs were long and lean, her face angular, not round and sweet any more like the little girl of yesterday. Small breast buds pushed against her shirt, hardly visible, but there when you looked. And now this manner of Mary's, this defiance.

A few meters across from her father, Grace thought of ways to kill him. Her bare hands would clearly not suffice, given the showdown of the previous minutes. What would it take to get one of those soldiers to plant a bullet between his eyes? She seethed, quietly.

She had to get away! Mary, his true target, would be home soon and Grace, having made the acquaintance of his fists for the first time, knew that in this new father of hers—a man who had newly stooped to throwing her across the room—lay an unbridled appetite for violence. If she ran she'd have to get away cleanly, and there was no sign of the key near the door. The security gate, that stoic soldier guarding the front door, offering a further level of protection from the evil world outside, now trapped her with the unaccounted for evil that lurked on the inside; that wildcard—a father; the threat from within, not factored into the metrics of safety for a home. She turned the word around in her head and for a moment wanted to stretch her hands out toward him, say "Daddy," and fold into his embrace like she did as a little child.

Patrick's eyes looked back at her, and when she searched them for cracks of love, they glinted like granite.

Footsteps up the garden path. Grace tried to lurch to her feet, but in a second Patrick had grabbed hold of her.

His voice was a sliver of a whisper. "Move again, and I'll hit you so hard you won't know your own name."

She sat down like an obedient dog. A deadly silence spun around them. They could hear Mary on the garden path, humming a tune. The clock on the kitchen wall ticked through the seconds, each one bringing Mary closer to the door.

Grace surrendered.

"That's my girl," said Patrick. And he smiled at her.

Chapter 9

Patrick had not gone back to his old home with the intent to inflict violence. He had wanted to talk—had wanted to tell Mary one last time to stop this foolishness. She needed him, he needed her; and now, with the police going crazy and soldiers everywhere, the child needed him too. He had been a bad father, a worse husband, but his instinct to protect those entrusted to his care had grown stronger as the country descended into madness. He needed another chance to make this right, to take up his place as head of the household, protect them. Johnny was gone, probably dead, though no one dared speak it. Grace could be next. The bastards didn't care that they were children. It was war, and everyone was a target.

He had meant to wait outside until Mary came home, but then he'd caught a glimpse of the child as she returned from God knew where. What the hell was she thinking? The Casspirs were swarming everywhere with their deadly cargo, ready to shoot in a moment. And here she was, idling about like someone with no cares, a vacant look about her. Was she that stupid? Patrick knew the girl could be slow at times, clever with book stuff, but just downright stupid with pure common sense. He blamed himself for that. He had left too much of her care to her mother. If she were a boy, he would have taken a much firmer stance, toughened her up from a young age, forced her to think about the world. But she was a girl, and he'd reckoned she would be okay as long as she followed the rules of the house. He had not taken into account this danger, this sickening threat of death that now hung in the air every day.

How was he supposed to prepare a child for this, to survive this? In a sense, he was grateful that she was a girl. Less likely to be noticed, less likely to be at the front of the protests, less likely to be marked as a student leader. But some of the older girls were going at it just as hard as the boys, shouting and screaming and marching like men, imagining they were someone. Not his Grace. There she was, standing outside the front door with that lost, faraway look in her eye, not even fully conscious of what was going on around her. Like a fucking lamb walking to its own slaughter. It infuriated him—this innocence in a time of evil. It deserved scorn. Punishment. Teach her to be awake, look around, know what's coming. He'd do it.

His approach was perhaps too forceful, his grip on her too hard. He could smell her fear. It excited him. At the same time, he abhorred this weakness in his own flesh. He wanted to shake it out of her. Wanted to tell her to walk erect and proud, and not put herself in harm's way in the first place.

He pushed her inside the house after her fumbling with the key. He would wait there for Mary, talk to her, tell her that this needed to end. They needed to be together.

Mary's appearance through the front door brought a rush of emotions that surprised Patrick in their intensity. Patrick knew these things: that he loved Mary with all his heart but that with all his heart, he hated her too; that he had been with her so long he could not conceive of a livable life without her in it; that children were lying dead, their cold bodies on concrete floors in unknown back rooms, unclaimed, unloved, unkeened over. He knew that their deaths hung in the air like a sickly perfume, choking him, smothering him, inescapable; he had been doing his best to avoid the Casspirs, knowing that his rage against the soldiers inside would not be contained were he to chance upon them, that such an encounter would certainly mean death.

When Mary walked through that door, it was like seeing her for the first time.

Crouching next to the girl on the couch, his hand taut across her face, the silence as Mary unlocked the security gate and then the front door. Her surprise, then fear—a sickening look. It was him, Patrick. Why did she have to act that way? He was not a monster. She tried to look strong, to steady herself, but her lips had always been her weakness. The familiar quivering top lip, which had the unfortunate effect of both shaming and arousing him, and with it the irresistible desire to plant his fist there, right on the sweet, quivering spot, where her full top lip started to curve down.

Her low voice, soothing, calming. Trying to talk him out of it. Why couldn't she have been like this before? She knew he had the upper hand now, knew she had to speak nicely to him and not scream and nag. Her hesitation, then coming over to sit next to him on the couch, to talk him out of it, talk him down. Sullen black eyes, giving him nothing.

He doesn't remember how. But then there is blood. Dripping down his right hand, pooling in the cuff of his shirt, the spicy, metallic smell of it overpowering him. Blood on his face, the front of his shirt. The child looking at him with uncomprehending liquid eyes, eyes standing still in her head. Unblinking, unmoving.

Mary, in his arms, shouting his name. Hitting the floor, him entangled with her. "What have you done? What have you done!" A pool of rust spreading below them, outward, lapping against the contours of her face in minuscule tidal waves.

Mary. Mary. Life was spilling silently all around them. Mary in his arms, light as a feather. Beautiful Mary with coal for eyes and perfect throat, skin the color of tea. The letting go. Her beautiful throat. The darkness, blanketing them forever.

Chapter 10

For the rest of her life, those few minutes will inhabit Grace. Sometimes she is right back there, eternally in that present, choking on the rusty smell of blood. At other times those minutes are a song stuck in her head, unshakable, drumming out the beat to which she marches along to life. We all have our crosses to bear.

For many years, the unfolding of events remained blurry. At first she remembered nothing. Then, gradually, images, smells, sounds swam back into consciousness the way a photograph slowly gives up its secrets after being submerged in developing fluid. Once fully recalled, they would come unbidden, in and out of her mind, floating, arriving, leaving, coalescing. Her will had nothing to do with them appearing or disappearing. Sometimes, when Grace tried to summon them, they wouldn't come. At other times they'd converge upon her, threatening to overpower her and shred all coherence. Then they would collapse like a deck of cards, scattering across the empty chambers of her mind. There was forever after a sense of confusion, a slippage when, just as the mind got to that moment, it would reel, retract, and skip a few frames, jumbling everything. Her mind could never fully grasp that day, could never hold on to the fact of what had happened. But as years stretched by, moments of lucidity shone through more frequently.

She remembered the crunch of the key in the security gate, the pause while Mary swung it open, the fumbling for a second key to the front door, seeing her mother's shape on the other side of the dimpled glass. Mary's head was bowed as she entered, and no amount of willing her to look up on Grace's part made her take in the scene before it was too late. When Mary finally did look up, shock scuttled across her face like a cockroach scurrying from the light. Her eyes darted from Grace to Patrick and her head jerked back a little.

"Why did you let him in?"

The accusation would haunt Grace for the rest of her life.

But we all have our crosses to bear.

Mary could still have run at that point, retraced her steps and walked right back out the door. She could have gone to the neighbors and asked for help, walked away and never looked back, but they all knew, Patrick most of all, that she would never leave her daughter; not with this crazy, wild-eyed man holding his old Okapi knife to Grace's throat.

"No, Patrick, no." Mary's voice was a raspy whisper.

No movement or sound followed. Patrick was breathing heavily like a man who had finished a long, hard race.

"Come over here, Mary."

"Patrick, please, we can work this out, Patrick. Put that away, let's just talk. Please."

"Now you want to talk?"

He gestured toward an armchair for her to sit down. She put her handbag down and slowly walked toward her husband and child.

"Close the door."

Mary turned, and in the moment Grace willed her to run, get the hell out. She wanted to reach out, scoop her mother up, and fly right out that door, over the rooftops and into the future, but the lead in her veins refused flight. Mary shut the door with resignation.

"Now lock it."

"Please, no, Patrick. Don't do this."

She started to sob, her hands pressed against the pane of the door in supplication to some unseen force. She turned back around, rummaging through her bag for her bunch of keys— taking longer than necessary, shaking.

"Patrick, leave Grace. Let her go. Please. Let's just talk for a while. Just you and me."

"Lock the door!"

She obeyed, grinding the key in the lock one final time, turning time and the narrowing trajectory of her life with it.

"I'm sorry, Patrick. I'm sorry. You were right. Let's try again. You move back. We'll get married again, what are papers...?" Tears streamed down her face, smudging her lipstick, making her mascara run, distorting her face into that of a clown. "Shut up. Shut up, Mary!"

She whimpered, quaked. Grace had never seen Mary like this before.

"Come and sit down. No, here. On the couch."

Mary obeyed, walking demurely past Grace and taking a seat next to Patrick. The whole happy family on the couch, thought Grace.

"See what it has come to, Mary? See what you make me do? My own flesh and blood? Why didn't you listen to me?"

Patrick relaxed his grip on Grace and turned his full attention to his wife. Mary exhaled, folded her hands on her lap and fixed her gaze on him.

"Put that thing away, Patrick. There's no need for that."

"No, Mary. No. You are not telling me what to do any more. Throw me out of my own house. Won't let me see my child. Who do you think you are, huh? Just who do you think you are? I worked for this. Worked for all of this around you, so you can dress in your expensive clothes and enjoy the way men look at you. Look at you! Painted whore!" He slammed his fist into his thigh for emphasis.

On and on, Patrick's mouth moved. Words circled like vultures in the air. Grace's eyes rested on the knife—a short knife, looking smaller than it had felt a few seconds ago against her throat. She stared at it, fixing her entire being on it, willing it to fall out of his fingers and under the couch. Against the backdrop of the dirt-mottled brown carpet it would be dull—not this electric, living thing recklessly flicking its tongue each time Patrick moved.

The shouting grew louder. With his left hand Patrick gripped Mary's shoulder. Tears fell down her face, her expression a silent beseeching: please, don't hurt me. Not again. She, who had finally found the courage to leave him, to say Enough! Yet he had forced his way back, back into the house, back in charge, a powerful body coiled to deliver retribution.

Fingers tracing Mary's lips, roughly, smearing the bright red lipstick all over her face. Evidence of her depravity, her disloyalty.

And then, a sharp painful breath is forced into Grace's body, exploding in her chest. A blinding shock of fresh air shakes her so that she finds herself, for the first time in her life, fully awake.

In swift, staccato movements, Patrick plunges the knife into Mary: one, two—sharp, precise movements, and it is over.

He has shut up, finally.

Mary falls forward, her eyes a wounded question, *Why?*

Her lips are moving but no sound escapes.

Then he's on top of her, cradling her before her head has a chance to hit the floor.

"Mary! Mary!"

Grace sits, stultified, as her parents sink onto the floor, grotesquely intertwined. Lying on the floor like one person, it seems both of them are bleeding from the same wound. Her father's hands are cradling and stroking Mary in the most tender of movements.

"Mary...." A softer calling, an affirmation. A recognition. Grace should have felt something. Fear, sadness, hurt.

Something.

But there was nothing, nothing to fixate on, nothing to look away to, nothing to grasp onto. It was as if she was swimming underwater, unable to make a sound. Then she broke the surface, gulped in air, and screamed. No words, just animal sounds. She dropped onto the floor next to her mother. Patrick had moved away from her. He was at the phone, holding the receiver in his hand. Grace screamed and screamed for her mother to hold on, as she tried, desperately, to staunch the blood from the gash in Mary's throat with her hands.

After all of the years of torment, of being scared, watching their step, calibrating Patrick's moods, staying in line—every little thing they did to avoid his wrath was meaningless. In the end it took a mere moment of him being God to snuff out Mary's life, and the rest of Grace's life with it.

Chapter 11

Everyone except Patrick attended the funeral. Although Mary had not seen the inside of a church for years, the pews of St. Thomas's overflowed with neighbors, colleague, and women with whom she'd gone to school. Patrick's father was there, too, skulking at the back, flanked by his remaining children. Why? Why—the question on everyone's lips. A woman in the prime of her life. A beautiful woman, as if the fact of beauty made it all the more tragic. In the days leading up to the funeral the neighbors, even the few who had liked Mary, had twittered under their collective breath about snobbishness, pride coming before a fall. With her nose always in the air, always thinking she was better than us. And now look—look how she'd ended up. Even at the funeral, while dabbing their eyes, these whispers spread like an ill wind, words gouging a festering wound. Grace heard them on the crest of the wind, heard them as they danced in dust devils, in front of her, around her. She heard the whispers subside as she came into sight and watched them fall dead at her feet. And although her mouth remained shut, she wanted to shout at them to shut up and leave her mother alone. Grace sat in the front row with Ouma, Mary's mother, as they wheeled the casket in, draped in a white shawl symbolizing Mary's baptism and rebirth in Christ. Yes, thought Grace, perhaps she will be reborn in Christ. She hoped so, but had doubts about Mary's suitability for heaven. But then a sick feeling washed over her as she pictured her mother in hell. Mary had not been to church in years, a mortal sin for Catholics, and had regularly cursed God. But she had had every reason to do so, thought Grace. Perhaps God would strike a bargain with her and allow Mary into heaven because of the raw deal He had given her, and the way He had allowed her to die. Perhaps the shock and pain and betrayal she'd felt in her last moments were enough punishment for her own sins, and maybe

He was allowing her now to rest in peace. If not, Grace reasoned, perhaps her purer soul could be traded for her mother's hopelessly stained one. Right there in the church she made a pact with God that from this point on, she'd live a spotless life in exchange for Mary's redemption. Grace would take on her mother's sin and go to hell in her place when the time came. If Jesus had washed away the sin of mankind, maybe Grace's blood would be enough of a price for Mary.

Ouma held Grace up, bracing her. Ashamed, the mother of the murdered woman didn't know where to turn her eyes, swollen red with grief. The neighbors must be whispering—oh, what they must be saying! Ouma knew some of the difficulties her daughter had faced in life, but even in her death, she could not come to terms with them. Haughty, prideful...and now look how she had ended up. She must have done something for a man to go berserk like that. The shame, the shame of it all.

The priest waited to greet the swaddled coffin at the altar while swinging a thurible, filling the small church with wafts of myrrh. The incense pressed down on Grace like an invisible hand in the center of her chest, setting the room off into a dizzying spin. As the casket came to rest at the altar, a low moan swept up from the back of the church. As it broke over the rest of the congregation, it went into full-throated sobbing. Grace turned and found the source of the wailing. Rowena, her face planted into Tim's shoulder, sobbed and heaved. Johnny was still not home. Johnny. His face was just a blur now to Grace who, despite her best attempts, could not summon it. She had completely forgotten about him until this moment. Now the image of him escaped into irretrievable memory, a place she used to visit in another distant life.

And her mother was gone, into the same void as Johnny, to a place with no coordinates that no amount of love or no unbearable longing could bridge. What was Mary doing? Was she cold? Was she happy? Would Grace ever see her again? Was Johnny there too? Where was Patrick? It all became too much for her. She closed her eyes and willed herself to move to the top of the room against the church ceiling and fly beyond.

When she opened her eyes again, the giant incense hand still constricted her throat. The priest was going on about how he had married them, how Mary had been a good Christian woman then but had moved away soon after. But it was not for them, mere humans, to judge. That was God's work. For no one could know the state of Mary's heart, nor her relationship with God. Perhaps in her final moments she had repented and found peace. Grace knew this not to be so. No one had asked her about those moments, despite the knowledge that she had been witness to them—no one wanted to know what she had seen. Those images were hers to carry, hers alone. We all have our crosses to bear.

Friends of Mary's, people Grace had never seen before, stood up and told stories of a kind girl with a golden heart, someone who always stood up for those weaker than herself. They talked about a girl who loved animals and painting and beauty. To Grace this woman only vaguely resembled Mary. She tried to imagine her mother as a girl her age. She had never thought of Mary before as a child who had harbored dreams, who had wanted to be something in the world, not just somebody's wife or someone's mother. The thought loosened her. Grace started to cry, first softly, then in huge, heaving sobs. Something took possession of her body as she shook and wailed. The incense hand dropped and her body broke free. She cried and cried and cried—for the young girl Mary, for the woman she had become, and for what had happened in between. She cried for Johnny, for Patrick. She cried for herself, alone and forsaken by every single star in her personal cosmos. Others joined in the wailing. The chorus grew in strength and built up to a majestic, weeping crescendo that rolled until it was truly spent and all that was left in the stuffy, smoky church were a few muted moans. In the silence that followed, the priest prayed for Grace. He asked God to look after her, to bless her and keep her always on the right path. The congregation affirmed him with a roof-raising Amen, but Grace did not hear it.

Part 2
1997

Chapter 12

The sky turned from gloomy grey to dark blue as Grace hurried along the pavement. She reached a gate and mounted a steep staircase leading to the front door of her home, barely stopping to scoop the contents out of the wooden letterbox attached to the gate. Bills, bills, flyers for a new restaurant down the road, the weekly specials at Checkers. She rummaged through the mail as she lumbered up the stairs to the bright green front door. Before she entered the house, Grace turned and paused to take in the twinkling lights of the harbor. Welcome home, they seemed to blink in a silent language only she understood. Grace never tired of reaching the top of the steps and taking in the view as night threw its veil across the sea.

As Grace exhaled the day, she fingered the gold cross in the hollow of her throat. She was exhausted. With a swift crunch of her key, she unlocked the front door and stepped into the freshly painted hallway. Almond Butter was the color she'd settled on. David had laughed indulgently at her vacillations between different shades of yellow.

"Grace!" he shouted from the next room. "Hello, love," she replied, absentmindedly.

She flung her coat onto the bench beside the door. Then she dumped the clutter of papers she'd retrieved from the letterbox on a polished table. A plain white envelope she hadn't noticed before peeped from underneath the pile of junk mail. She picked it up.

Grace de Leeuw.

The envelope was addressed to her—in her maiden name—the handwriting unfamiliar.

No one had addressed her by that name in the two years since she'd married. Heat rose into her cheeks.

The envelope bore the stamp of the only post office in the

place where she'd grown up. The heat spread across her chest. She didn't know anyone there any more—hadn't been back since the day she'd left, after her mother's funeral. She turned it over. No sender's name, no address.

"Hey, Gracie!" David called again.

Grace stuffed the envelope deep into her brown bag, the one she wore to work each day, and left it on the bench. She'd deal with the letter later. She took a deep breath, composed herself, and strode down the long hallway, peeling off more layers of winter clothing as she went. By the time she reached the living room, she felt as if she'd shed her skin. Crouching down on her haunches, she scooped up the baby from the blanket on the floor.

"Hello, Sindi!"

She cooed and cuddled and kissed, inhaling the fragrant folds of her daughter's neck, nuzzling her chubby cheeks, grazing the infant's curls with her lips and planting kisses on the palms of her tiny, fat hands. She felt anchored. She was home. Sindi was growing daily, visibly; every new day brought a new skill, a new small facet of her personality.

The baby gurgled in her arms, smiled, and promptly threw up.

"Let me help you." David, who had been watching the daily reunion, laughed. With a few swift movements he was up from his seat at the dining room table, brandishing a cloth with which to wipe the vomit from both mother and child. He pecked Grace's cheek. In the large kitchen, which flowed into a living room, he had already lit a fire, and a pot of stew simmered away on the stove.

Good old David. Always ready to help, always cleaning up after her. He was always happy to see her, always cheerful in his welcome, and always efficient in balancing Grace's moods with the growing responsibilities of fatherhood.

"Have a good day?"

Grace nodded, although her husband didn't wait for much more of a reply from her before launching into the details of his own day. She listened absentmindedly as she got back down onto the floor with Sindi.

"...been marking since I got home from school. I'm very worried about the matrics this year..."

David had this way of making his day sound like it had happened at the center of the universe. Grace made sure to look up and smile at appropriate moments as he narrated it all—the threatening rain in the morning, picking Sindi up from daycare, the conversation with the day-mother about her teething, what he'd decided on for dinner, the school prep he needed to finish by tomorrow.

Sindi babbled along with her father.

"Sit with her, Grace, while I make us some tea. And I think she needs a nappy change...."

Grace let the words slide off the invisible bubble she had constructed around her and her baby daughter. When she was at work, Sindi's absence was a physical ache—all day she longed to stroke the brown curls, nuzzle that pudgy neck, and inhale her child's sweet baby breath. By midday her breasts were painfully engorged. Pumping them took an entire lunch break, a wasted hour that could have been better spent with her child instead. She loved work, but resented the time away from her daughter. She held Sindi tightly against her body, trying to create a private world for just the two of them. Sindi's cheek against her neck was a relief; the balm she had been craving all day. At the sink in the kitchen, David chattered happily about his day.

They had married two years earlier after a courtship spanning their student lives.

Grace had laid eyes on David on their first day at the university —that venerable intellectual home of the left—as they stood in a snaking line around the registration building to sign up for their courses. The line reminded her of one she'd stood in for hours the year before, to cast her vote for the first time. She had turned eighteen a few years before, yes, but this was the first time she could vote; it was also the first time Aunty Joan and Ouma got to make their crosses.

Grace felt a similar excitement lining up to register, although it was a much more mundane line. Nevertheless, it was a line that would stake out the future of each person standing in it. It was the beginning of the rest of their lives. For the first time in its history, students at this institution were lining up to register as free citizens in a democratic country. They were free, liberated by Nelson Mandela and the ANC. The promise of a university education, on top of the vote, inflated even their most extravagant hopes.

There was nothing they couldn't accomplish now, no limit to the imaginings of what they could be. They were free. Free! The very air around them was nectar, sticky with expectation, almost too sweet to breathe.

Grace fell in with a group of girls and was laughing with them when she noticed David, and noticed him notice her. She tried to avoid his eyes—she couldn't bear to be looked at by men. Or anyone really. To function in her world, Grace needed to fade, not stand out nor attract attention. Things were safer that way. Nobody seemed to notice or care about a shy girl who didn't say anything. No one expected her to have much to say anyway. But David didn't stop looking, and as the hours wore on and the line barely moved, he seized the opportunity to shuffle up a few spots in the queue until he was next to her.

Blocking her off from the group in which she'd tried to blend, he introduced himself with the confidence of one who had always been listened to and launched into a conversation that felt like it had been left off the day before. She liked him immediately. His voice was warm and strong, and they fell into an easy conversational rhythm—he talking, she listening and interjecting every now and then. His strength and surety warmed a strength inside her that she hadn't known she possessed. She had been anxious about starting this new part of her life. Her biggest fear was that someone from her old life would recognize her. The university bordered the township, which seemed to Grace, through the bus window, as depressed as ever. By the looks of it, democracy was yet to arrive on those streets. If any of her former neighbors had made it here, she'd rather not know them.

She worried about not making friends, about sinking further into that well of loneliness with which she was far too intimately acquainted. Her high school teachers had prepared them for university, stressing that it was nothing like school. One needed to have opinions, to make oneself heard, sometimes in a lecture hall of hundreds. Here it was ideas that counted, not learning things by rote. Grace knew how to study and memorize things —words, dates, and passages—but she didn't know what she thought about things. She had been feeling hopelessly inadequate even before entering the university gates.

But the excitement in the line and the carefree laughter and chatter had loosened her. She didn't trip over her words when David spoke to her and was immensely grateful that he chose her to sidle up to. Emboldened, she sparkled at him.

David put her at ease. He asked questions, but none of them too probing, and freely gave information about his life and family. She envied this freedom, but carefully concealed her envy. Together on that first day they had explored the campus, discussed class options, and compared their rosters, which conveniently overlapped at more than a few points. They ate a late lunch together in the enormous cafeteria, a modern contraption with a side wall of glass that made Grace feel as if she'd stepped into the future. Taking in the vast landscape from that huge window, she'd realized with mild surprise that she felt at home, that this was a place where she could breathe. Amidst hundreds of ambling young bodies she was anonymous, invisible, free. And yet there was this intimacy with her new friend, a kind boy with an open face, that made her feel a little less alone. For once, Grace felt good. She felt normal.

Over lunch she gave David the story she told all new acquaintances when they bothered to ask: her parents had died in an accident when she was young. She had been raised by her mother's sister, Aunty Joan. Usually no one pried after this, and David was no different.

Outside the cafeteria there were ancient trees, a well-kept lawn, and a deep blue sky with only the slightest wisps of cloud. After lunch, Grace and David basked in the sun in companionable silence. In the distance, she made out the shape of the airport control tower, a monument to a different lifetime. How things had changed. No more burning tires, no more petrol smoke polluting the air, no more violent deaths for young men (for young women it was another story), no more disappearances. The things that had happened over there, so close to that airport, were a closed chapter of her life, buried deep inside of her. As always, the thought of Johnny came unbidden, as it did whenever she felt happy or sad. How he would have loved this place. Had he ever come home? Grace had never had the courage to return to her childhood home to find out.

As the day drew to a close, she felt sad at the thought of parting with her new friend. So this was what people meant when they said it felt as if they'd known a new acquaintance their whole life. Grace was telling him things she'd never before thought of sharing with another, things she didn't know she had inside of her to give, about paints and new worlds and colors. Things that would have sounded stupid to anyone but David, who lapped up every morsel she shared. She liked herself in David's presence; she had things to say and opinions to voice because he asked, and listened, to her replies. At the end of that day, she boarded a bus with him, pretending that she was going in the same direction, even though she'd have to take an extra train back home to Aunty Joan's. She had wanted their conversation to last forever, to spread into the night, the next day, the next week.

Since that day she and David had been together. They had moved seamlessly from friendship to relationship to marriage. At twenty-seven years old, they were the loves of each others' lives, as they liked to tell each other and everyone else. They were blessed to have found each other so early. Some of their friends limped from one dysfunctional relationship to the next. After graduating, they'd both found good, decent jobs—David as a teacher, Grace as an assistant to a director in a large financial corporation.

There was a year in university when Grace dreamed of writing poetry—especially after discovering a flood of recently unbanned books written by people like her—or at the very least a writer for a newspaper. She might not have expressed herself very easily, but she thought about things deeply. If she were given a chance, she thought, she would be able to express her ideas well on paper. Instead she kept a notebook, in which she surreptitiously practiced writing down her thoughts, along with the odd poem. But no one she knew had ever made a living at that, and she didn't know where to start. So when she'd been offered the chance to make good money as a personal assistant, her first ever job interview after she graduated, the brown notebook was consigned to a bottom drawer in her dresser. Thinking and planning on behalf of someone else, always being one step ahead of him—that was her job. She found it exhausting but pleasing. She had a purpose; she was contributing to this new society. And soon there was her family to care for too.

Grace tickled Sindi and laid her down on her stomach. She was nine months old, and she needed time on the floor to strengthen her spine and forearms so that she could learn to crawl. Grace had read all the baby books and knew every age-specific milestone Sindi was supposed to reach. It bothered her that she had not yet started crawling. She needed to crawl in order to walk— Grace was anxious for her to grow up healthy and happy.

David asked her again about her day, but what was there to say? She'd had a perfectly fine day, the same as every other day before it. She had taken phone calls, booked a conference venue, arranged meetings for her boss—all in all an adequate, smooth-running day once she had thrown herself into it. Why bother boring him with it all? She shrugged. "Good," she told him.

Since Sindi's birth, Grace was aware of how withdrawn and moody she had become. She missed her mother. Unable openly to tend to the wound that had reopened with her daughter's birth, she'd taken to snapping at David. She knew it was unfair, but sometimes she couldn't stop herself. Tonight his small talk chafed more than usual. She wanted to be alone; needed time to think. And uppermost in her mind was the white envelope she'd stuffed down into her handbag. Who could have sent her a letter, mailed from that post office? And how had they tracked her down?

David got that cautious look. She'd only been home five minutes and already she was tense, irritable. The more he tried to engage, the more she pulled away. The effect was predictable, and it made them both uncomfortable. The more Grace withdrew, the more animated David became. It drove Grace insane, him babbling away like an idiot, hoping she'd thaw a little more. It had the opposite effect, but he couldn't seem to help himself.

"Uh-oh! Out of milk for our tea. Let me run down to the café and get some!" The relief in his voice was palpable. Grace looked up from the baby and smiled at him, but made no comment. He clanged down the hall—"Back in a bit!"

Grace echoed his relief when the front door closed behind him. A wave of guilt followed. Why did David always have to be so damned cheerful? Her mood seemed to foul in proportion to his eagerness to please. While she hated this quality in herself, she didn't know how to change it.

With David gone, Grace made sure Sindi was in a safe spot, then dug into her handbag and took out the envelope. She flattened it against the table in the entryway and stared at it. She still didn't recognize the handwriting, but this letter could only be from one of two people: Patrick or Johnny. Both spelled trouble, a spilling of the past into her present. She brought the letter to her face, put it to her nose—nothing was revealed by sniffing it. On the verge of opening it, she lost her nerve and stuffed it back into the handbag. There her fingers latched around the familiar shape of a slim cardboard box. She had started smoking again —a habit she had picked up in her last two years of high school. After checking that Sindi was still okay on the floor, Grace moved stealthily out the back door into the small courtyard behind the house where, through the window, she could still keep an eye on the child, who was lying there wriggling contentedly. Grace struck a match and lit the cigarette, inhaled deeply as she closed her eyes, and savored the way the warm smoke traveled through her body, loosening its kinks. After the first calming puff, she pictured the smoke filling her lungs, circulating through each limb, passing through every membrane and into her bloodstream. In her mind's eye, tiny particles of poison trickled from bloodstream to breast into breast milk and flowed through her milk into Sindi's innocent mouth. She sighed as she exhaled a cloud of smoke. She detested this habit of hers, but she didn't know how to stop.

The smell of the cigarette mingled with the aroma of David's stew on the stove, creating an acrid stench. And suddenly Mary was there. Grace saw her leaning over her pots, a wooden spoon in one hand and a cigarette tipped daintily away from the food in the other. Mary could come like this, unbidden, in moments Grace least expected, evoked by the smell of ginger or the sight of a rose, bringing a smile at first and then a longing so fierce it felt like a hand squeezing her heart. Grace sucked on the cigarette as if it was her dying breath. When she was done, she wrapped the stub in a tissue, went back inside, and flushed it down the toilet. She scrubbed her hands, brushed her teeth, and ran talcum powder through her hair to remove any lingering traces of smoke. She stuffed the cardigan she was wearing at the bottom of the laundry basket and changed into a clean outfit. By the time David reappeared with a carton of milk, she was smiling happily from the living room floor, Sindi in her arms, the picture of maternal bliss.

They ate lamb stew for supper, in silence, while Grace bopped Sindi on her lap. After dinner Grace cleaned the kitchen and then she scooped Sindi from David's lap to prepare her for bed. First they played a little on the bed, cuddled together, and then Grace bathed and fed her, marveling, once again, at the most beautiful creature she had ever seen. She rocked Sindi and sang to her softly, feeling a guilty relief when David settled down in the next room with a pile of marking. Tonight she'd have Sindi to herself in the last hour before sleep claimed her. Tucked up in bed with the child, Grace whispered a story about a girl who was so adored by her mother that she plucked the moon out of the sky and presented it to her as a gift. She held Sindi close and watched her eyelids slowly droop across the full moons of her large brown eyes.

When David next appeared in the bedroom, he gently removed the baby from the bed and placed her into her crib. Grace stirred, looked up at him, and gave him a sleepy smile. How lucky she was; how far away her life had moved from chaos to peace. She could not have asked for a better partner in life. It was as if the gods had decided that she had suffered enough and had granted her these gifts to blossom in love—a husband who would cheerfully die for her, and a beautiful daughter who had infinitely expanded her capacity for love. Grace resolved, for the millionth time, to be more cheerful, more grateful. To be kinder to David. To stop smoking. She hated the grip of this addiction, hated even more that she was harming Sindi's health through it. Grace had read the books, knew the statistics and correlation between pregnant mothers' smoking habits and cot death. She hated this secret that lay between her and David.

Secrets. And now there was another secret nagging at her, one that had the potential to unravel a series of other omissions she had brought into their marriage.

The letter in her handbag could upend everything.

Could it be from Patrick, she wondered. But her father was supposed to be in prison for life. And wouldn't a letter from an inmate bear the prison's stamp?

Grace knew that the act of opening that envelope would open up a new world—or, rather, an old one, one she didn't want to reenter, and from which there might be no return to the contentment of today.

So could Patrick be out? They had not followed the trial proceedings all those years ago, and Grace didn't know what the sentence had been. She had just assumed that he would be locked away for life. He had murdered a woman, after all. But with talk about amnesties in the air, who knew? What she did know, though, was that she did not want to hear from him. She didn't want to know. You are dead to me, Patrick de Leeuw, she thought. You died long ago when you murdered my mother. She wasn't about to let him ruin her life a second time. What would David say? The whole childhood she had invented for him was a lie. Grace wanted Patrick de Leeuw not to exist, and as long as she left the letter unopened in the bottom of her bag, she could pretend that he didn't.

Grace was wide awake when David crept into bed beside her. He rubbed her arm. She turned away. He tried again. "You still didn't tell me how your day was," he said.

"I did tell you, David. It was utterly uneventful."

Chapter 13

Mornings were always a wrench. After a night of fitful sleep interrupted every two hours by Sindi's wailing, Grace rose to feed a hungry, whiny, living alarm clock, who renewed her protest as dawn broke. David heard Sindi's cries, half opened an eye, rolled over, and went back to sleep. Grace had a grudging admiration for her husband's ability to snooze through it all. To be fair, he had also been woken every two hours, but he always found it easier to get back to sleep. He would have helped were Sindi bottle fed; he'd even begged Grace to switch to formula feeds at least some of the time, so they could alternate the feeds. Grace was the one who insisted on breastfeeding whenever she was not at work. He had stopped trying to change her mind after a while. "This is my baby; it's the least I can do for her," Grace insisted.

She held the infant to her breast, allowing her to feed. Sindi was teething, and while her disposition was friendly during the day, night times revealed a different little personality. After feeding Sindi, Grace burped her, as David's mother Gwen had shown her to do. The rhythmic rubbing of her back soothed the child. She settled into quiet gurgling as Grace placed her back in her cot. Finally a few minutes to steal a shower.

"Watch her, David?"

David grunted, and satisfied that he was semi-awake, Grace showered and got dressed, with one eye on the crib. Her beauty regimen consisted of a shower, deodorant, and throwing on what-ever clothes were reasonably clean. No blow-dryers or lipsticks or coordinated accessories for her. Ready for the day, she set about packing the baby's bag, putting in several changes of clothes, nappies, Sindi's favorite plush stuffed duck, and a small cooler with bottled breast milk.

David stumbled out of bed and into the shower.

Sindi had become clingy over the past few weeks. It was normal at this age, the day-mother, Val, and the baby books had re-assured them, but Grace couldn't help imagining her daughter stuck in a playpen all day at daycare. Now it was Sindi's turn to be dressed. Grace changed a soiled nappy and put a fresh baby-gro on her. Sindi had more outfits than her mother, which was just as well, as the cold required layers of clothing. Grace tried to stuff the child's arms into a padded jacket—Sindi balled her tiny fists and gave a low, discontented moan, which escalated into a full-blown wail. Her limbs stiffened; Grace could feel the anger in her tiny body. Sindi thrashed from side to side, her protests growing louder and louder.

"It's okay, baby," Grace soothed. "I don't want to leave you either, but you have to be a good girl, okay?"

Sindi vomited her reply. Grace felt like screaming too, but restrained herself, undressed the screaming baby, and started again with a fresh outfit.

As he did every morning at seven o'clock, David took Sindi and all her baby paraphernalia, kissed his wife goodbye, and sped to the day-mother's house to drop off their daughter. They were hardly out of the front door when Grace dragged herself out to the courtyard to settle the frayed edges of her nerves with a cigarette. She had failed again. Failed as a mother—her daughter was unhappy—and failed to quit smoking. She could feel the addiction sinking its greedy claws deeper and deeper into her. She despised herself for that grip. It was freezing outside, but she stood in the cold, filled with self-loathing, and inhaled the familiar mix of anger and self-pity along with the comforting smoke. With each inhalation, she cataloged life's injustices against her—the things that drove her to smoking. If she still had her mother, life wouldn't be so difficult. Sindi would have a grandma to look after her, instead of being shipped off to some stranger's house every morning at the crack of dawn. Her baby was missing so much; she would never know her grandmother. Grace was missing so much too. How do you mother without your mother?

They had been married for less than a year when she became pregnant with Sindi, or as David put, "we" became pregnant. It annoyed Grace, the presumptuous "we." She had not thought about whether she wanted children, had not planned the pregnancy, but when it happened, she had wanted the baby more than anything. She had wanted this one little thing to herself: the acknowledgement of that hallowed space between mother and unborn child. It was a miracle: she was growing this baby inside of her, with her own blood and musculature. Something of Mary was going into the child too. She could feel its flutters, its kicks and hiccups that woke her at precisely four o'clock each morning. She didn't say anything to David, allowing him to "we" away, but it grated on her. She longed for the space to just feel something, for once, her way.

By that time, Aunty Joan had died and, being childless, had left everything she owned to Grace. They used this modest inheritance to buy a small house in the formerly grey neighborhood bordering the city, now increasingly fashionable, overlooking the bay. And just like that, they had it all—the house, careers, the baby on the way. They were a couple on the move, part of the all-important, new black middle class; drivers of the economy of the new nation. They settled into domestic bliss: married, happy, respectable—thanks to the new South Africa and Aunty Joan's generosity. They had it all. But was Grace happy? She didn't know. She observed herself detached, as an outsider would, and felt that this would be what happiness looked like. Did she feel it? She didn't know. Grace navigated the world with a thick, invisible membrane wrapped around her. Very rarely did anything touch her. She was present, but not there. The old survival tricks of Saturn Street were near impossible to discard.

During pregnancy, Grace nursed silent, brooding fears that had no outlet now that Aunty Joan was gone. It had not been that long ago that she herself was a child, and who would teach her the things about a baby that only a mother could? There was nothing she could remember from Mary that could be used in her own child-rearing of an infant, and Aunty Joan, although loving, had not been particularly maternal. Nor had she prepared Grace for domesticity. Grace could hardly cook when she married David. She fretted and worried throughout the pregnancy about the baby's health and whether she would be a good mother. What if it died, like her long ago brother who had been stillborn? What if there was something wrong and it needed a lot of medical attention?

Her biggest fear, the thing that gnawed at her in the small

hours of the morning, the thing that woke her in a cold sweat, the thing she couldn't even admit to herself by daylight: what if she didn't love it? What if it was born perfectly healthy and beautiful, but she felt no connection to it? What was the magical thing that makes a mother instantly fall in love with her baby, and what if Grace didn't have it? And then, the wound at the center of it all: what if she was like him? What if she had it in her to hurt her own child, to take its life?

She could not, dared not, share any of these concerns with David, who was happily expecting. Her lies had gone on for too long and stretched too far back. What would he think of her and their marriage if he knew the truth? That his wife was the daughter of a murderer; that she was also a skilled liar.

The prison Patrick had been sent to was on the outskirts of the city. Grace had never visited him, not once. She was not allowed to speak his name to Aunty Joan, or any of the few family members she saw from time to time as the years went by. It was as if Patrick had died too, and in her mind Grace had buried him along with her mother.

The first year after it happened, she had lived with Ouma, Mary's mother, who deposited her, straight from the funeral, in a tiny room at the back of the house with only a bed in it. It was neatly made, and it had a tufted cream bedspread. Ouma had tried, but the room lacked warmth. It was painfully bright, sterile; white walls and no curtain, since the window faced a small courtyard and needed no screening off from prying eyes. Grace lay down on the bed and simply disappeared into it. Even now, as an adult, she recalled very little of those days after the funeral: not the season, not the weather, not the music on the radio that year, not even her mother's face (that would come back a few years later). She didn't remember eating or washing or changing clothes. All she would later remember was the whiteness of those walls. The schools had effectively shut down the last few months of that year, so there was no need to get up in the morning. There was nowhere to go. Grace lay in bed for days, wanting to cast her eyes on nothing else but those walls. It was as if her eyes had seen enough for three lifetimes and wanted to rest. The blank space of wall, infinitely white, became a canvas on which she could project herself and rest—it was the only thing preventing her from ripping out her hair or gouging holes into her skin. As she lay on the mattress staring at the walls, nothing came, not a single thing, to her mind. The whiteness stared back at her, overwhelming her and bleeding into her, along with the hollow light of loss and pure grief. The blankness suspended her in life when death beckoned. If Grace could have found the energy to kill herself, she'd have done so during those days in the white room. In their utter blandness, the white walls somehow kept her alive.

For whom, for what, was her grief? Her mother, yes, but also for so much more than that. What could have been—the warmth of a family; the order of mother and father as protectors and nurturers; the indestructibility of the unit; the loving home. The white space of the room erased with finality all of these possibilities. Blanched, parched, Grace lay on the bed facing it while cursing herself; fighting against being subsumed by the enervating blankness, yet feeling held by it too.

Grace had no memory of how long she lay like that, but there came a day when Ouma entered the room, pulled her out of bed, and smacked her. She swung Grace's legs off the bed, lifted her chin with her hand, and turned her piercing eyes directly onto her face.

"Your mother is dead. She's not coming back. But you are alive," she said. "Live!" She paused for a second to let the words sink in. "If you don't, I will send you away to a home."

Grace collapsed back on the bed, feeling the first flutters of a will to return in her chest. Yet she didn't know how to take back command of her limbs and her voice. The weight of Ouma's expectation made its home on her chest, and she sank deeper into the bed, with eyes too heavy to open. A doctor came to see her and prescribed vitamins and rest. Grace would come out of it, in her own time. But Ouma had grown tired of her.

A week later Aunty Joan arrived. Grace had seen pictures of her, but this was the first time she remembered meeting her mother's sister. She packed all Grace's belongings into a weathered suitcase she had brought with her, and bundled both Grace and the suitcase into her car. Almost no words were exchanged between Joan and her mother. Whatever war raged between them came to a silent truce so that Joan could enter the house and collect Grace.

"You're coming to live with me," was the only thing Joan said on the five-minute drive from Ouma's house to hers. Grace wondered why they hadn't just walked, and later she would also wonder why Joan never visited Ouma's house. She knew why she'd never come to Saturn Street though—Patrick had banned her from setting foot in their house. But that day in the car, with the huddled-together houses whizzing by, was not the day for questions. The answers would come only years later.

Grace walked into Aunty Joan's two-bedroomed flat and marveled at the sufficiency of her space. Joan had a comfortable, neat home. Art and framed photographs adorned almost every wall. Here was a young Mary framed in gold against an orange wall; there a picture of a chubby baby she recognized as herself. There were pictures of Ouma and Oupa, and of Joan and Mary as young girls. Grace was amazed that someone she'd known so little about—they were not allowed to mention Aunty Joan's name in front of Patrick—had traced, with photographs, a full family genealogy, Grace included, against the walls of her living room. The frame in which Grace's baby picture sat was embellished with delicate, lace-like flowers. It warmed her that someone had put thought into choosing a frame in which to put her image, one that matched a detail in the dress she was wearing in the picture. Aunty Joan had thought about her and had cared enough to display her image with obvious care.

"Sit down."

Grace obeyed, and Joan disappeared into the kitchen, emerging minutes later with a slice of chocolate cake and two glasses of Oros. Grace devoured the cake feverishly, ignoring the cake fork on the plate and digging in with her hands. She licked every crumb and every scrap of icing from her fingers, something Mary would never have allowed, and surprised herself by asking for a second slice. Joan laughed quietly and told her no, she could have another piece later on, one was enough for now. They sat across from each other in silence. The suitcase stood unopened at Grace's feet.

"I live alone," Aunty Joan said then. "Have done for years. You're welcome to stay—I've got enough space." She gestured around the room. "But if you don't want to, I'll take you back to your Ouma later today."

Grace looked around. The sun was splitting shafts of light on the wooden floor. No dirty carpets. No dirty anything. For the first time she looked at her mother's sister directly. She looked nothing like Mary. There was the same thick, curly hair, tied back in a way Mary would never have condescended to, but other than that, nothing. Joan wore no makeup or jewelry. Dressed in a simple cotton blouse tucked into a long skirt, she was like a moon to Mary's sun—she emitted a cool glow to Mary's amped up heat and painted lips. Her eyes were softer, calmer, without those desperate, erratic flickers of light in her mother's that Grace loved and loathed at the same time. Here was a woman who did not need to be seen, who didn't need to have her beauty validated to feel alive.

"I will stay," Grace declared, as if she had a choice.

"I'm glad. I was hoping you would."

They sealed the arrangement by finishing their Oros together in silence.

The first thing Joan did was buy Grace new clothes—loose shirts and pants that were easy to get in and out of and easy to clean. Grace had never been allowed to wear clothes like these at home. Joan gradually got rid of Grace's stuffy, frumpy clothes. Mary had loved her little girl as a copy of herself, and Grace had never objected, but the high-necked chiffon blouses Mary favored for her inevitably sent her into a hot and sweaty mess. Mary's clothes stifled, whereas Joan's freed her up.

Then one day Aunty Joan brought home giant strips of canvas, procured from an artist friend, along with oil paints and brushes. She moved all the furniture in the living room against one wall, and sat Grace down in the middle of the room with these supplies, giving her one command: "Paint!"

Grace tried to protest about not knowing how, but Joan assured her that it didn't matter.

"Just paint a picture for her or about her. It doesn't have to look like her. You know abstract art?"

Grace didn't, and Aunty Joan explained that all she had to do was color the page with her feelings. There needn't be lines or recognizable shapes; Grace should let the paint take over and let the feeling of it guide her to tell a story.

"Let the colors and textures lead you. Play with them. Feel them. You don't have to stick to the brushes. Use your fingers, your elbows, your feet, if you like."

No one had ever told Grace to play before. She struggled to let go of herself but slowly, gradually, after weeks of Saturday afternoons sitting on the newspaper-covered floor and allowing the brush in her hand to lead her, she settled into it. Grace relearned breathing. Week after week, her canvases lightened from somber greys and blacks to radiant swathes of green, yellow, and ochre. Is this how her mama had felt when she'd made her paintings all those years ago? She wished she had Mary there beside her to ask. But when she got lost in this world of color and smell, the loss of Mary felt, for moments, bearable. Gradually the moments of bearing it moved closer and closer together, like pearls on a string, until there were hours and then whole afternoons when the loss didn't rasp at her.

She never kept the paintings, was happy to let them go off with Aunty Joan. Once they were done, Grace was happy to release them and the feelings embedded in them into the world. She didn't feel ownership or a need to cling. She learned, without language, catharsis; a blessed release that moved things through her, and the events of that dreadful day away from her, so that Mary's death became a part of her life without obliterating her. Joan offered little instruction during these forays onto the canvas, leaving Grace alone with the brushes and tubes.

One afternoon as she knelt beside her to help gather up the newspaper after a particularly long painting session, which Grace had started in gloom but completed with a contented glow, Aunty Joan smiled at her and said: "Never forget what you did today. You created something. Don't ever forget that you have that inside you, the ability to create an entire universe out of nothing. I did it. You just did it. We all have it in us."

Grace didn't understand what Aunty Joan was on about. She had made a color backdrop on a page and then overlayed a few squiggles on top, adding, for the first time, white paint over dried orange, and here Joan was calling it a universe. She said nothing, and because she'd loved the sound of Joan's voice as she'd said that, smiled obligingly at her aunt.

Slowly, very slowly, under Joan's hand Grace came back to

life. Joan was not an overly affectionate woman, and never again would Grace hear the words "Grace, darling" or be covered with a multitude of butterfly kisses in a fit of affection. But nor would she be frozen out and ignored when the tide turned. Joan had an abiding calm about her, and in her presence Grace felt calm too.

On rare occasions Joan would tell stories of Mary as a child, how she loved to paint, how her eyes had an insatiable hunger for color. Mary could take a simple geranium flower and get lost in the universe of its hues. Joan's eyes went soft, but her mouth turned down at the corners when she told such stories, and as much as Grace loved to hear them, she never pressed or asked. She grew adept at the art of waiting for these tales. To her they were beautiful gifts that would drop from Joan's lips at the most unexpected times. Grace would listen, breathlessly, trying to take in every word. This was the mother she had never known, as she was before Grace existed. Mary had lived independently of her and had loves and passions that had nothing to do with her. The thought saddened and enlivened Grace. In these moments she learned so about her mother that she hadn't known.

"She told me she loved painting. I always wondered why she didn't do that at our house."

"Well, she was busy looking after you." Joan was quick to defend Mary.

"She always told me how much the boys loved her."

"Yes, they did," Joan laughed.

As the years stretched by, stories of Mary became less sad and more celebratory. They remembered the best in her: her humor, her wit, her great beauty. The other things were locked in a room of Grace's heart that she never examined.

During the last months of her pregnancy, Grace worried about this fractured knowledge of an absent mother. Would it be enough for her to find her way as a mother? She ached for both Mary and Joan, and felt freshly bereft.

Her worst fears dissipated with the first breath her daughter drew. Grace fell absolutely, unequivocally in love the instant she laid eyes on Sindi. Never in her life had she seen anything more perfect than the puffy pink face or felt love's tug more insistently than when the baby's chubby hand curled tightly around her little finger. Sindi was perfect. Perfect. She brought a flood of love into Grace's life. Sindi was the current that pulled her further along into safety, further away from that day. Grace's experience with love was that it always came with a price—you gave up a little of yourself, always, in order to get the love you wanted from people. Not so with Sindi. No part of her was diminished or relinquished by loving the child. Grace felt she could give and give and give again of herself without feeling used or depleted. Sindi brought peace, a feeling that she could live in this world, with each breath a gift, as long as her daughter was in it. With Sindi nestled against her, each moment was complete unto itself, needing nothing more than two pairs of eyes gazing into each other. The rhythm of her baby's breath, the seasons of her sleeping and waking, became the metric by which Grace structured her days.

When Sindi was five months old, Grace reluctantly returned to work and life took on a different cast. Already tired from waking every two hours to feed at night, she found being away from her daughter for nine-hour stretches excruciating. She began to retreat deeply into herself, but when venting her anger and grief was unavoidable, she found a convenient target in David, who rapidly learned the art of tiptoeing around a sorrow he couldn't understand. Outbursts he could deal with. It was the unrelenting, moody silence, the irritated flash of an eye, the sullen turning away from him that left him floundering, babbling, following Grace around like a dog seeking a kind word from its master.

What she would give to have one more day with her mother; one more hour with her daughter and mother, together.

She nipped the thought along with her cigarette. Better not to go there. She still had to put in a full day's work. After straightening the kitchen and liberally spraying herself with perfume, she set off for work in the city center.

As she waited on Main Road for a taxi, it became clear after a few minutes that no taxis were running. A fellow commuter explained that the taxi drivers were on strike and said that their best option for getting into the city would be the train. The train station was another fifteen-minute walk away, but with no other options presenting themselves, Grace joined a group of taxi-less workers trudging down to Station Road. Soon she found herself jammed in the middle of a carriage, swaying along to the sounds of the morning commute's symphony with a host of unfamiliar warm bodies on their way to work. Within minutes the train had unloaded its bustling cargo in the heart of the city. Grace disembarked and wove her way through throngs of commuters, scuttling like ants, in and out of Cape Town station. She flowed with the mix of people exiting the station concourse and came out into Strand Street, which was alive with bodies and cars intent on getting where they needed to be with maximum speed. She still had time for a quick coffee, which she bought at a stall on the Parade. She had a quick smoke too.

The energy of the city lifted her gloom. Some days she still couldn't quite believe that they had won, had voted, had overcome. With the dark days of Casspirs, teargas, and bullets behind them, the city belonged to her now. Grace felt part of its lifeblood, flowing along its arteries, bonded to the army of workers that made it run smoothly. She loved it, and it loved her back. As she walked along Darling Street, the city opened up to her. It throbbed with life, flirting with her, welcoming her—a muscular lover, energetically wooing her.

At work she took her accustomed seat behind the huge glass desk with three different phones. She made notes on her desk calendar of everything she'd have to do by noon in order for her manager, Mr. de Vries, to have a successful shareholder meeting in the afternoon and depart to the airport for an overnight trip to Johannesburg. Catering was confirmed; reports had been copied and collated; the driver for the trip to the airport had been confirmed. She made sure of his reservation at his favorite hotel and booked a late dinner for two at a new steakhouse he'd been wanting to try. His wife wasn't accompanying him on this trip. Grace tried not to think about his dinner companion. She had set up no dinner date with any business associates.

Mr. de Vries was already in his office with a partner. He was a wonderful boss—demanding but always courteous, often playful, and adored by all the women in the large company. He started his work day at 7:00 am, but after her return from maternity leave, insisted that Grace only start work at nine. Maintaining a strong bond with her baby was crucial, especially in the first years, he had told her. Grace was to stick strictly to her working hours—he could manage on his own early in the morning, especially since he used that time to get uninterrupted work done. Grace could have cried when he'd sat her down to tell her this. She had been expecting some kind of complaint about the quality of her work. She tried not to let it show, but her work—her very life—was suffering from lack of sleep. They had settled into a new routine after this conversation, Grace with renewed gratitude and adoration for the man.

At 9:15 sharp, Grace entered Mr. de Vries's office with a freshly brewed pot of coffee and a stack of messages she'd retrieved from his answering machine.

"Morning, Grace," he nodded cheerfully.

He had a visitor with him this morning. The man looked at her and gave her a brief nod, eager to get back to the business at hand.

She left the office, pausing just outside the door to pick up a note that she'd dropped.

"Not much to look at," she heard Mr. de Vries's visitor mumble.

And then the reply: "Dull as dishwater, I'm afraid. But it's just as well. Removes all temptation—wouldn't want it right under my nose."

The two men chuckled. Grace moved away from the door as quietly as possible. She only allowed the tears to come in the safety of the bathroom, after she had wiped and packed away the tray on which she had served their coffee. Dull as dishwater. That's what wonderful, kind Mr. de Vries thought of her. Through her tears she looked at herself in the bathroom mirror. She had struggled with the baby weight, and her slim waist had not returned after Sindi's birth. Her skirt, which she noticed was faded, was coming undone at the hem; her cardigan was creased. To her horror she spotted a stain Sindi's bout of vomiting had left on her cardigan. How had she forgotten to wipe that off, or change into an altogether new outfit? The biggest mess in this ensemble of ungainliness was her hair. Before Sindi's birth, she had gone once a week, just like Mary had done, to the hairdresser for a roller set and blow-dry. David liked to joke that you could tell the day of the week by the state of her blow-dry: from Monday's loose buoyant curls which by Wednesday had lost some of their bounce, to limp Friday strands best bunched into a ponytail. On the weekend the hair cycle would start all over again. God help

David if he suggested anything that interfered with her time at the hairdresser's. After Sindi, this luxury had fallen away, though, along with money for new clothes. They were middle class, yes, but only just. Sindi's birth had swung them precariously to the lower end of middle class, so even their once a week nights out became a fond memory.

Grace took in the full calamity that was her hair. It hadn't been cut in months, hadn't felt the soothing warmth of a blow-dryer in weeks. She had smoothed it over with some pink oil, but it was winter, and the morning mist had "activated" her hair like nothing in a bottle could. Her curl coiled up from her head in an unruly, frizzy mess. For the millionth time, she cursed her father for having inherited his hair instead of Mary's smooth locks, which withstood every type of weather. What a curse Patrick was, even now. No wonder everyone found her ugly. She was his child, after all.

Her thoughts turned back to the letter that was still unopened in her bag. Was it from Patrick? Well, fuck him, if it was. And fuck Mr. de Vries too. If only he knew how easy it would be for her to accidently mix up receipts for his wife's and various girlfriends' gifts. Cheating swine.

She cried again for a little while, then composed herself and went back to her desk. The rest of the day passed in a coffee-fueled blur, for which she was grateful. Before she knew it, she was back at Cape Town station deciding which train to catch home. Three main arteries ran from the station to the different sprawling suburbs of the city—the southern line to the affluent southern suburbs and south peninsula, the northern line to the Afrikaans-speaking north, right up to the Boland; and in the middle, the line that transported the working class to the Cape Flats. It didn't matter which line she took—all the trains passed her destination station before they branched off and snaked their way across the metropole to deliver their cargos to vastly different lives.

Grace looked at the board—the next train leaving was on the Cape Flats line, and she sped to the designated platform. A rushed, unfriendly guard clipped her ticket at the turnstile. She had exactly one minute before the train's departure. She broke into a jog to get to the third-class section on time. She jumped into an overcrowded carriage just in time, pushed through the mass of people, and sank down onto the bright orange seat. A wave of exhaustion crashed over her. Please, God, let Sindi sleep through tonight, just this once. She tried to empty her mind, but her thoughts kept gathering around the letter at the bottom of her brown bag. Like a loose tooth, it worried her. What was she to do? Burn it? Shred it? Open it? She sighed as the train rolled out of the station and closed her eyes, mindful of staying awake for the short journey to the next station, where she would disembark.

As the train gained speed, a blind man shuffled through the carriage to the rhythm of "Guide Me Oh Thy Great Redeemer," which he sang while banging a tambourine. His sidekick, a boy no older than twelve, followed in his wake, stretching out an inverted hat. Grace pretended to be asleep as they passed her, but the hymn had a calming effect, and she kept her eyes closed, giving herself over to the rhythmic movement of the train.

Grace could tell by the jerking movements of the carriage that they were nearing her station. As the train slowed to its final halt, she forced her reluctant eyes open, and there he was, right in front of her: Johnny.

Chapter 14

Was this another vision? She'd been seeing Mary a lot since Sindi's birth. Was Johnny up to the same ghostly tricks as her mother? Was this a conspiracy of ghosts to pull her to the brink of sanity? No, no. This Johnny was flesh, breathing before her and staring at Grace in that quiet, intent way she remembered well. He was not the Johnny she had summoned a thousand times to her mind; time had clearly left her hand on him. The eyes were deeper set, with fine lines feathering the skin around them; his skin darker, but still freckled in that boyish way. They sat there, frozen, staring at each other without any movement between. The train shuddered to a halt, and Grace rose, gathering her bags, without taking her eyes off him.

"Grace."

She saw him mouthing the word without a sound escaping his lips.

"Grace!"

This time he spoke her name into the air filled with the warmth of strangers' bodies. The train stopped, the doors slid open, and the crowd rearranged itself as more passengers entered. Grace started toward the door, then turned to give him one more look. He was getting to his feet. She moved on and stepped out of the train, onto the platform, where it was already getting dark. She turned again, and there he was behind her. She faced him as tears gathered in her eyes. They stood motionless, each probing the other's eyes, until the train pulled off and disappeared around a bend. Johnny was here, in front of her. Real. Grace's head spun as she grasped fruitlessly for words.

"Is it you?"

An unnecessary question, but one she felt compelled to ask. "Is it you?" she implored again.

"Grace! Oh my God! Yes, it's me," he laughed.

The sound of her name in his mouth dislodged decades of holding it all in, keeping it all together. Grief and relief flooded her body, rushed to the surface of her skin and poured out in an incoherent jumble of words and tears. Reserve snapped. Words clattered across the concrete of the station platform.

"What happened...where were you? Why? Why didn't you find me?"

Johnny. Johnny. Johnny.

Tears were streaming down her cheeks. Johnny was laughing and crying too.

"You are alive!"

As she uttered these word, an awareness grew that at that very moment, she, too, felt alive, maybe more than she'd ever felt before. His name was that first breath you take after holding your head under water for a long time; the first shard of daylight after a dark, horrible nightmare.

After ages, he replied simply: "Yes, it's me. I'm alive, Grace."

Words bubbled from her: how she thought he was dead, that they'd killed him. How she couldn't bear it after her mother.

His hands moved onto her shoulders, steadying her shivering body.

"No, I didn't die, as you can see. They kept me for a while—I came out of detention after three months."

"What did they do to you, Johnny?"

He shook his head slowly while smiling his sweet, gentle smile.

"It doesn't matter now, Grace. It doesn't matter. That was a lifetime ago."

"But why? Why didn't you let me know? You must have known I was worried, that I cared...."

Her words pierced the air; her whole body had become one big question, greedy for answers. "Didn't you know that I cared?"

"By the time I came out you were gone, Grace."

"Why didn't you look for me? Why didn't you find me?"

Grace thought of the years she had spent at Aunty Joan's apartment, long days of obsessive trips to windows; looking out, scanning the streets, waiting to see him walk up to the front door. Or days when she'd be walking down a busy street or strolling on the beach—how she would endlessly scan the crowds. And then the sudden flicker of hope at the sight of a boy with a familiar build, a certain height, a certain type of curl at the nape of a brown neck. Once she had followed a boy through the city on a Saturday morning, trying not to be noticed but desperately keeping him in sight until she could see his face. Grace had looked for Johnny everywhere, seen him everywhere and nowhere, until all hope forsook her, and she gave up wanting him back. But she had never quite shaken the reflex of scanning a crowd. It became like breathing, this scanning of men a certain age. And here, on a day when she hadn't been looking, he'd appeared.

"I was right here, Johnny, all these years. Waiting, praying. I waited for you every day. Why didn't you find me?"

The question had hardened into reproach. She knew it was unreasonable—they had both been children when he had disappeared, and nothing bound him to her.

"I thought about it, Grace, God knows. But when I came back home, you were gone. I wanted to look, but nobody knew where you were. They said your grandmother had taken you away. And anyway, I didn't know if you wanted to see me."

"Of course I wanted to see you!" Grace was crying again.

He gently clasped her arm and led her to a bench on the platform. A soft evening fog enveloped them as they sat, Grace trying to steady her breath, Johnny thoughtfully rubbing his hand, as if rehearsing an important speech in his mind.

"I thought about you every day," he finally declared. "I wondered about you, wondered how to go about finding you. I heard about your mother. And I wanted to see if you were okay. I know how close you were...."

Grace felt the fog around them seep into her head, swirling there in a murky despair. He knew about her mother. Of course he knew; they were right next door.

"But honestly, Grace, I was in a bad way when I came out. It was hard to find myself again, let alone someone else. Those were not good years."

Her heart, so used to breaking, broke again at these words. They had both been broken, in very different ways: Grace by the man of their house, Johnny by men heading a different order; but all of them, men who needed ruthlessly to control, to snuff out rebellion, to keep the putrid peace in their respective regimes. Men who didn't brook dissent. Men who had been revealed as fearful cowards after the protective armor of violence had been stripped from them.

Sitting now, close together on the bench, after the initial deluge of words and tears, both Grace and Johnny had lost their tongues. She had so many questions. What had happened to him in prison? Grace's mind got caught on the fleshy image of a man called Benzien—the malignant name had stuck with her—whom she'd seen on TV just the previous week, demonstrating to an audience the everyday evil he had casually sown. She had snapped the TV off, not wanting to have even an echo of that monster's past in her home, her space. How many Benziens had Johnny encountered? And what had he lost to them?

It was almost completely dark when Grace gathered her stuff and got up to leave.

"Do you live nearby?" She nodded, yes.

"Let me walk with you. You shouldn't walk alone in the dark."

They walked together in silence, through the subway, onto a little side street, and up the hill toward Main Road. Droplets of mist suspended in the glow of streetlamps clung to their hair and coats.

"You know, Johnny, you were my only friend." He smiled but said nothing.

"Besides my mother, I had no one but you. You don't know this, but you made life bearable for me."

They walked on in silence, but as they got closer to her street suddenly Grace didn't want him near her house, near David and Sindi. Johnny symbolized her old life. He was a living, breathing ghost from her past, and she didn't want him contaminating the new.

"I'm okay here, Johnny, I'm just a few streets up. I can make it alone."

He nodded, stopped on the corner and awkwardly patted her shoulder as she turned to continue on her own.

"Grace!" he called, after she had progressed a few steps. "Do you have a pen? You look like an office lady."

She noticed then his steel-toed boots, the same type her father used to wear. Grace dug in her bag and handed him a ballpoint pen.

"And a piece of paper?"

UNMAKING GRACE

After scratching around for something for him to write on, her hand fell on the hard edges of the unopened envelope. She pulled it out, briskly folded it over to hide her address, and handed it to Johnny, who scribbled something on it, then held it out to her.

"This is my number. It's my home number. Phone me. I'm home after seven, usually. I'd like to keep in touch."

The envelope hung in the air between them for a few moments. Secret upon secret, Grace thought. What was she letting into her life? The past was racing faster than she could run, insisting on making its presence felt. She took the envelope and stuffed it back into her bag.

"Really. Phone me."

She nodded. "Goodbye, Johnny."

Grace turned and walked up the damp, dark hill without looking back.

David was frantic when she reached home, bombarding her with a series of questions while holding a crying, writhing Sindi. The baby seemed to be reproaching her too. Grace apologized, blaming the taxi drivers' strike, and scooped both of them into her arms, soothing ruffled feathers.

Soon anger and worry had dissipated. She and David ate a simple supper of roast chicken, and the nighttime routine swallowed the rest of the evening. In bed Grace tucked herself snugly against her husband, who had, for once, turned in early too. Her arm crept around his waist, first gingerly, then pressing him toward her. She buried her face in the back of his neck. She sensed the shock in his body—Grace was always needing space, always finding ways to needle a little bit of distance between them—then felt him relax into her. He sighed contentedly. She sensed a question in him but felt it dissipate as she pulled him in tightly toward her. She knew she had been difficult for David, who was always kissing, stroking, needing touch. Grace found such demonstrations of affection stifling, an invasion of her body, even more so after Sindi's birth and an endless need for her mother's body. She was always holding, bathing, stroking, nourishing the child, and David's physical needs were too much after days of having her body colonized by this little person. Her husband had been starved of physical affection, Grace knew, guiltily; and at the times when she could bring herself to bear his advances, she had a habit of folding one arm tightly across her chest, as if to preserve some little part of herself.

But on this night, the night of Johnny's coming back, she needed David, wanted him with a physical hunger that surprised her. Inhaling his sweet, slightly musky smell, she banished the day's events from her mind, as he turned, folding in toward her.

That night the house on Saturn Street permeated Grace's dreams. In her nocturnal travels, she walked up to the front door, frightened, knowing that an important task awaited her inside. Sindi was in the living room—she could see her through the big front window—and Grace needed to get her out as quickly as possible, but as she reached for the front door, it shifted out of her grasp. Several times she woke, drenched and breathless, only to fall asleep and back into the same dream, while David slept like a baby.

Chapter 15

Here is the thing about living a secret: you have to have the stomach for it. Some people thrive on the little charge they get from doing something illicit, something not even those closest to them would suspect. When Grace thought about it, she knew that her father must have been such a man. Grace, however, was not a woman who could live a secret. It was one thing to leave the past where it belonged, but when it came back in the form of letters and people? No. Those kinds of secrets were too heavy for her, and the thing at the bottom of her bag, the thing which had now doubled its danger with the scribbling of a few digits on its surface, gnawed at her. She could not quite believe David had said nothing when her face must so clearly have spoken of her guilt. The knowledge of what lay in her bag pulled her spirit down; made her wonder what the hell had possessed her to keep this thing, the defining thing about herself, from David. Her father was a murderer. He had murdered her mother, yet her husband had no idea. The father of David's wife, the grandfather of his daughter, was a killer. What if this thing was genetic? What if Grace had it in her too—didn't David have the right to know? Would David still love her if he did? There was not only that, the murder, but also the lie. She had told him that her parents had died in an accident. Even if she came clean about it now, what would it say about her that she had been with David for years and had not entrusted him with the truth? David was a lovely man, a gentle man. Grace had known, instinctively, that if she had told the truth before their marriage, it would not have changed his feelings for her. He loved her deeply, this she knew. The facts of her childhood would probably have made him even more protective of her. This struck Grace as his weakness: his goodness, and his belief in the innate goodness of others. David had not seen the ugly side of life as she had. The childhood he'd described to Grace was happy and uneventful. The worst trauma he'd experienced was his father dying at too young an age, of a heart attack. That loss had sealed his relationship with his mother, Gwen. She was one of David's primary confidantes. He did not know the propensity for violence that lay just beneath the surface of every human being, even those closest to us; had no idea of the intimate cruelties that could inhabit the architecture of a life. He had not been hurt in that way, ever, by those he held dearest. It made him vulnerable. He trusted and depended wholly on Grace, a trust unreciprocated by his wife.

Although she loved David as much as she had loved any other person in her life, Grace had never fully surrendered herself to him. She carried within her the silent knowledge that she would be able to walk away from him at any moment if needed. Grace had had a backup plan since the day they promised fealty, a plan she could execute if she ever needed to leave: a bit of money stashed in a bank account he knew nothing of, extra sets of clothing for her and Sindi in a drawer she could empty in one minute with the sweep of a hand; ID book and bank card securely stored; cash tucked in an envelope at the bottom of another drawer. If needed, Grace could disappear with Sindi in less than ten minutes and never have the need to look back. Or so she thought. David was innocent of these things she kept in shadow. Although he was very much the head of the household, the back door from the marriage that Grace left ajar gave her a sense of control, a feeling of having the upper hand. A woman should always be with a man who loves her a little more than she loves him. Grace could still hear the authority in Mary's voice as she'd imparted this bit of advice. Grace believed it, even though Patrick's brand of love had gotten her mother killed.

Sometimes this need for control shamed Grace, but she needed it all the same. It gave her a measure of comfort with being owned, in that peculiar way marriage allows, by a man. Aunty Joan's advice had contradicted Mary's. As always, they had different approaches to the question of men. Joan had drummed it into her: never be dependent on a man. Make part of your life your own, so that you'll be able to walk away if you need to. She didn't have to say the unspoken, that Mary would still have a life had she been able to do this.

The weight of Grace's old and new secrets grew daily, strangling what little vitality she had left out of her and waking her in the middle of the night. Should she tell David about her father? What would he think of her? And what about Johnny? In her mind, Grace's life had been sharply delineated by her mother's death. Everything she knew before that line had inexorably been drawn through it had disappeared or been taken away from her: her mother, her home, Johnny, even her clothes and little treasures collected as a child. On the other side, she had spent most of her life longing for these things: Mary, Johnny, a feeling of home. She had gone some way in creating a home and a family with David, but there was always the ache of some essential part of her missing. Her mother, obviously, but Johnny was tangled into that loss in ways Grace couldn't always unravel. Now he was there. It was just like him to walk back into her life on an unassuming night. And although she didn't want her life disrupted by what was done and buried, she longed to see him again. God, he had survived those desperate years. Grace wanted to know how. She felt an excruciating need to know his story and to share hers with him; to stand their stories side by side and enmesh them like the twin helix of a strand of DNA.

She thought about how to welcome Johnny into their lives. Invite him for tea? Introduce him to David? The thought of them meeting was like a brick to her stomach. How would she explain Johnny? If she introduced him as a childhood friend, David would bustle with questions about what she had been like, what they'd done together, which parent she most strongly resembled. David had tried a few times after they were married to excavate some happy memory, surely she must have had some—but she refused to speak about her parents at all. The few pictures she owned of them revealed young, smiling faces unaware of what life held for them, entranced with each other. She had offered these reluctantly to David along with a portrait of Mary which had been prized while she was alive. In it, Mary shone. David had remarked on Mary's beauty, stirring the old discomfort in Grace. There was the gold cross, Mary's, which always dangled around Grace's throat. David had never seen his wife without it.

If Johnny came onto the scene, old questions that had been laid to rest would start churning again, burning their way through the placid surface of Grace's new life. No, she could not afford to let the two men meet.

But she needed to see Johnny again. She wanted to hear everything she'd missed, wanted to know whether she'd left a hole in his life the way he had in hers. A week after their reunion on the station, Grace felt herself digging in the bottom of her bag for the envelope, soft by now from her pawing. She had touched it often, feeling it again and again for some kind of reassurance that Johnny was real, that she had not just imagined him on that train. One afternoon she waited until after the work day, when everyone was gone from the office. She pulled out the envelope and smoothed it out. Then she lifted the phone and dialed the number that was written on it. A woman answered. Was it Rowena? Of course not—he wouldn't still be living with them after all these years. The voice on the other end of the line called his name, and there were muffled sounds as distorted voices floated to Grace's ears. She almost slammed the thing down. What was she doing? What did she want from this man? Then his voice came through, clear and immediate, and she smiled, happy to hear it.

"It's good to hear from you," he said, after preliminary greetings. "I was hoping to hear from you."

"It's good to hear your voice too," she said.

Then what? They were happy to hear from each other, happy to once again be within reach of each other, but what else was there to say, beyond that? A tenuous past bound them, much of it belonging to the territory of the unspoken.

Johnny broke the silence. "It's hard to talk like this. There's a lot I want to say."

Grace nodded in assent into the receiver, as if he could see her. She liked his directness.

"Let's meet, Grace. Can you meet me for a drink one evening? Tomorrow?"

No, she couldn't. Not so soon. Grace wanted to see him but needed time to think. All of a sudden, it felt wrong to be making arrangements for a drink with what was after all a strange man. "Next week then. How about next Thursday?" Johnny said.

She was surprised by his insistence after all the years of doing nothing to find her, but she agreed—next Thursday would be good. That gave her enough time to think about what she needed to hear from him and enough time to change her mind, even though she knew at the moment of agreement that she wouldn't. They decided on a pub in a suburb close to her home. It would just be one or two hours, long enough to talk uninterruptedly and find what was to be found in one another. She would explain to him about David, how he didn't know about her past and how she'd like to keep it that way, paving the way for an introduction of the two with her secret still intact. It didn't occur to Grace that in setting this plan in motion she might be entering into a conspiracy of silence against her husband with another person.

Grace's week passed in a flurry of work and caring for Sindi. The baby was teething and kept her up every night that week. David was preparing his students for the June examination and worked late into the night, often collapsing into sleep on the couch in the living room. Grace hardly saw him and their communication dwindled to truncated conversations over hastily prepared dinners. Exhaustion cloaked her shoulders, but resting her tired mind on Johnny provided respite—a sweet savoring of the anticipation of seeing him again. Grace was aware of a deeper stirring; this pleasure was not entirely innocent, but she convinced herself that it was okay to be happy about retrieving such a large part of her lost childhood. Wasn't that what she wanted—to go back and rewrite her broken childhood? She shut off these meandering thoughts which became, after a few days, like treacle flowing through her brain, reassuring herself that it was her right to be happy to see an old friend. Grace smoked more, inhaling every doubt that crossed her mind with the diaphanous bands of smoke. Fear and guilt about Johnny and the past gathered into her throat, lungs and blood vessels, spreading like a drug through her body, along with the excitement at the thought of seeing him again.

Thursday arrived, and Grace was ready. She had told David the night before that she would be meeting friends from the office after work, a development he found odd, but didn't say much about. Grace was not one for finery, but on this night she wore her most flattering skirt with a fitted blouse buttoned to the throat. And as always, her throat was guarded by Mary's cross. She found some long-forgotten lipstick in her desk drawer, carefully applied it at the bathroom at work, then wiped it off again with a tissue. She left the office with a mixture of dread and delight running through her veins.

Johnny wasn't in the pub when she arrived. Grace got a small table and waited with her back deliberately to the door, so that she wouldn't appear to be desperately scanning each person who entered. For a moment, she prayed that he wouldn't come— that would solve her secrecy problems and relieve her of a growing sense of unease. She could go home, pretend that none of this had happened, that she hadn't met him on the train, hadn't arranged to see him behind David's back, hadn't lied to her own husband. She could get up out of her seat at that very moment and still walk away from a situation that would be difficult to explain were David to find her here. She looked up and Johnny was there, smiling, and it was as if he'd never left her side.

Over beer they closed the distance between then and now. They reminisced about how things were, remembering the neighbors, remembering how they used to lounge in the back yard when Johnny took a break from his garden chores to eat the sandwich Mary made him; Mary and how stern she was—funny recollections of being kids in an irretrievable, but still-present place. Johnny reminded her of the fun part of her life then, the innocence of the games they played and their grumblings about chores. He took her back to a place which was surprisingly sweet, reminding her that there had been more to life than just violence and chaos. He shared details about Mary Grace had forgotten. In that pub he resurrected Mary for a brief but magnificent spell, making Grace see her through eyes she thought she had lost.

"Don't call me aunty!" He did a bad impersonation that some-how had the right tone.

It was the first time Grace had spoken about Mary, had said the words "my mama" out loud in years.

Johnny teased her about her shyness as a girl, while confessing his awkwardness too, their laughter followed by silence as each one's memories jogged private recollections.

"Your father was very good to me," Johnny said. "The only man, besides Tim, who took an interest in me and, you know, guided me."

His tone was reverent, like a boy remembering a beloved, departed uncle.

Grace's mood soured.

"And what possible good advice could you have gotten from a murderer?" she said.

Silence fell between them in the space where just minutes before laughter had bubbled. Fury crept up Grace's throat, but she swallowed it.

After all the years, there was still the instinct to cover up, not to air the family's dirty laundry.

"He just snapped," she said. "I never understood how he just snapped like that, Johnny."

He faced her squarely.

"It's me, Grace. You don't have to pretend. I know what happened in your house long before your mother died. Everybody knew."

"Why didn't they help us then?"

"Well, it was your parents' private business. No one has the right to interfere between a man and his wife." He paused. "But no one thought he had that in him. I mean, if it was so bad, why didn't your mother just leave him?"

Grace remembered the question from childhood. Ouma, when they met that one time without Patrick's knowledge at the Wimpy for breakfast: "Why don't you just leave, my child?"

Mary never had an answer then, and Grace didn't have one now. She did try to leave, over and again, but see what had happened when she made her final move, once the divorce papers were signed? Grace felt the shame of it all, fresh as if it had happened yesterday, rise to her face.

Johnny ordered another round of drinks and changed the subject. He talked about Tim and Rowena, telling Grace how they'd saved for years and had finally moved out of the crowded garage. He still saw them, though they, like everyone else, were getting on in years.

Grace smiled, grateful for the change in topic. She realized they hadn't actually talked about his life, about the things that had happened to him during that terrible time when he went missing. She had no idea what Johnny had gone through. She was not the only one who suffered during those years.

"When you disappeared, what happened? What did they do to you, Johnny?"

Johnny's eyes clouded over. He took a deep gulp of beer and wiped his mouth with the back of his hand. A low, bitter laugh escaped his lips; his eyes refused to meet hers. Hurt lay shallow there. Grace regretted having asked the question, so soon. They'd only just found each other again. They faced each other wordlessly, the happy reunion now riddled with memories they'd both fought hard to forget. Grace wanted to know, and she didn't. She also wanted a smoke, and Johnny was happy to oblige. They moved outside and both lit up.

The night was damp, swirling with a centuries-old Cape Town sorrow. She leaned against Johnny's car, savoring the fragrant smoke and its calming effect on her body. Johnny paced before her, tracing an invisible line with his feet. He reminded Grace of a dog on a chain being pulled repeatedly back into his allotted space. He was so different and yet so similar to the Johnny she had loved many lifetimes ago. He looked up from his pacing and caught her studying him. They both smiled.

"I'm so happy to see you, Johnny."

He walked over to her in one giant step, encircled her with his arms and kissed her. Grace didn't fight it or feign resistance—she wanted this, wanted him. His body against hers, his lips on her skin felt like a homecoming, a sacred entry into a place toward which she had been journeying her whole life. His embrace unlocked her body and spirit. She opened to the world she had worked all her life to keep at bay; felt the energy of a million stars vibrate and flow through her. A weight flew off her.

They remained locked in an embrace long after the kiss ended. Grace realized that now that she had found Johnny, she didn't want to let go of him. A lonely car, lights dimmed by fog, crawled past them in the narrow street. Despite the cold, Grace's skin flushed. Finally, she broke the spell.

"I should get home. Please, let's go."

They went back inside, where Johnny paid for their drinks.

In the light of the pub, Grace couldn't bear to look at him.

Once outside again, he unlocked the car door and held it open for her. They made the short drive in silence, with Grace speaking only to give him directions. The car stopped outside the house which contained David and Sindi, Grace's whole life, everything she loved, and Grace felt something tear inside of her.

Can I see you again?" Johnny asked.

"No. No. We are never doing this again."

Grace jumped out of the car and slammed the door, damp air cutting into her skin. She ran up the steps to the front door, taking them two at a time, not stopping to look back.

In the warmth of the living room, David was crowing at Sindi, who was still awake way past her bedtime, while his mother, Gwen, looked on. Great! This was all she needed—her mother-in-law. Gwen loved lingering conversation, always asked how she was and genuinely listened to the answers. Tonight, Grace just couldn't. David and Gwen looked up and smiled as Grace entered and Gwen rose from her seat to kiss her.

"Grace! I haven't seen you in such a long time!"

As she kissed Grace's cheek, she instantly recoiled. For a few seconds her eyes held Grace's, filled with bewilderment. She looked Grace up and down until Grace could feel her skin burning under the older woman's gaze. Was it the cigarette smoke that clung to her, or the smell of another man? Gwen seemed to see through her. Had she guessed what had transpired just a few minutes ago?

"Are you feeling okay, Grace? You're burning up."

"No, Ma Gwen. I don't feel good. I think I've caught some bug." The two women had always adored one another. After Aunty Joan had died, Gwen was the only mother Grace had known. On the day she and David married, she had welcomed her into the family by calling Grace her daughter. The title sat uneasily with Grace, yet the affection between them was heartfelt, in many ways sustaining Grace as she moved from young woman to wife, to mothering. Grace admired the way Gwen had raised her son. David's steady, calm way was a testament to his mother's love and discipline. To be caught in such a sordid act by Gwen would plunge Grace into a place beyond shame. But here she was, full of love and concern, draping a tender arm around her daughter-in-law's shoulder and ushering her into the bedroom. Grace didn't deserve this.

"You're burning up, girl! Let's get you into bed with something to drink."

David stood in the doorway, uncertain, as Gwen undressed Grace like a baby, folded her clothes, and slipped a nightgown over her head. Being fussed over by an indulgent mother was not an altogether unpleasant feeling, but what did her body reveal to Gwen about her encounter with Johnny? Mothers always know.

"David," Gwen chided, "don't just stand there—make Grace some tea. With honey."

David nodded and bounced off to the kitchen, and Grace found herself in bed, with Gwen administering a damp cloth to her forehead. When David returned with her cup of tea, she tried to smile a thank you at him, but her face was stiff and unwilling. He looked remorseful, as if he'd caused whatever was going on with her. Grace stifled the urge to shout it all out, come clean about the man she had seen that night, about this man's connection to another: her personal set of Russian dolls—each harboring a secret that could end life as she knew it. Grace wanted to beg David's forgiveness and plead with him to help her make sense of all of this, to fix things so they could go back to the life he did not yet know was shattered, but none of the words churning inside of her seemed adequate. She couldn't find an entry point into her own story; didn't know how to neatly slice it into beginning, middle, and end. What would David think of her? And Gwen? Could they ever forgive her? Would they love her the same as they loved her now?

Her thoughts clung to the air like pockets of mist before a strengthening sun. She looked at David. She could hear his mother clattering around in the kitchen and talking to Sindi. He came over to the bed and kissed her on the top of her head, imploring her to get better soon. Grace wept, which made David fuss over her even more.

She slept fitfully that night and awoke some time before dawn, drenched in sweat, her body on fire. She ripped off the bedclothes to get some relief, dumping them in the space next to her where David usually slept. Her parched throat ached for water, but the glass swam out of reach as she tried to grasp it. The room contracted, spinning before and around her; its walls menacing closer, then jumping further back. A gust of wind out of nowhere, and there she was, Mary, next to the bed, looking down at her daughter. Grace tried to call her name, tried to reach out and touch her, but she couldn't move. Language had been snatched from the hollow of her tongue. There was no sensation in her limbs, just the burning, burning, while her mother wailed: "Talk to me!" Then Mary turned her back, gliding out of the room, gone, again. Grace found her voice: "Come back!" but it was David who appeared through the door. He rushed to her side and sponged her down again after wringing out the cloth in the bowl next to the bed. The night passed with Grace consumed by fever.

When she opened her eyes, they welcomed daylight, not fresh, tinted, new, but wrung-out, middle-of-the morning light. The house held itself in that singular, quiet way that signaled no one home—all she heard was the low hum of the refrigerator in the kitchen. She sat up in bed. Her nightgown was damp, and there was a metallic taste in her mouth, but her head was clear. She felt awake, alive. She got out of bed and padded through to the kitchen, where she filled up the kettle and turned it on for tea. Then she jumped under a cold shower while the water boiled. Under the painful thrust of water, she scrubbed herself pink, as the plug-hole drained the dregs of her secrets. A great deal of dead skin was shed. As she stepped out of the shower, drying her body until it tingled, Grace felt reborn. Once dressed, she threw open the French doors and stepped out into the courtyard.

This was it. A second chance. No more lying, no more secrets. A fresh mountain wind caressed her body, tugging at her wet hair. She sat down on the wooden bench in the yard and took in the magnificence of the mountain—why did she not come out here more often to glory in its shadow? Table Mountain was showing off, just for her, its lush peaks jutting up against the sky. On a crisp winter's day like this, it was dazzlingly beautiful and so close she felt she could reach her hand up and stroke its contours. She closed her eyes and imagined the woolly texture of the mountain against her palm—like touching the face of God.

She retraced the events leading up to her illness and found them light years away, so distant she felt unsure that she had even met Johnny. Perhaps he had been part of her febrile dreams. She felt sick just thinking of what had passed between them—a kiss on a pavement outside a seedy bar in Cape Town. She shifted the thought aside. This morning was new. Her body had been renewed. She grabbed the bright promise of the day and made a silent vow to herself, with Table Mountain as her witness: no more lies.

BY BARBARA BOSWELL

Grace sat for a while sipping her tea and savoring the solitude of the courtyard. Soon her stomach called her back to the real world—she was starving. By the time David walked through the door with Sindi, she had roasted some chicken, along with vegetables and rice fried with onion and tomato. She ran to them and threw her arms around both husband and child, never wanting to let go.

David was delighted. "You're better! You were down for days!"

That's how it felt, like she'd been gone for days, and now Grace was back and she didn't want to leave him or miss one second of their life together. She brushed his cheek with her lips; he smiled his puppy dog smile. They kissed some more, playfully, as they'd done in the early days before marriage vows and Sindi. Her silent promise to herself flashed through her mind. She would tell him the truth—everything. But later. Now she wanted this moment, his grateful smile, his strong arms around her, his hands traveling up and down her back. She would tell David later.

Chapter 16

The day was going badly, and it was not yet eight in the morning. Sindi had kept them awake all night, causing David and Grace to oversleep. Both were late for work, scrambling to get it together while the baby dolefully declared her need to stay home. Grace's heart broke, then hardened, finding a convenient target in David. She was angry—but with what? With David for not helping more, for not waking on time, with the frigid day for crashing into the intimacy of a night not ready to be over. She was angry at everything. Their goodbyes were terse, rushed. Grace left the house shortly after David sped away in his little car, taking Sindi to the day-mother. On her way to catch a taxi on Main Road, she stopped at the corner shop for cigarettes. It had been two weeks since she'd last smoked, since the day she'd made all those promises to herself. That part of her promise, the not smoking, that at least she'd kept. She hadn't yet found the right time to tell David about her father, about her mother, everything, as she had promised herself she would. Work was demanding. Sindi was teething. It could wait until they had some time to breathe. She had quit the cigarettes cold turkey for two weeks, but today she needed something, just one or two, to get her through this morning. At the counter she counted out her coins and settled for three loose cigarettes, not a whole pack, and a box of matches. Her head throbbed. She slid the coins across the counter and snatched the three cigarettes in return before darting out of the café and around the corner, where she could smoke in peace.

Huddled against a wall, Grace struck a match, cupping her hand as she brought the flame up to the cigarette dangling from her lips. She closed her eyes and inhaled, welcoming the first hit of fragrant smoke as it journeyed to the depths of her body. Her limbs loosened, her hunched shoulders fell back a bit and her headache dulled. A pleasant numbness crept over her body, and her brain mellowed to a calmer frequency. She exhaled, watching the plume of smoke stream from her lips. Relief. The smoke looked so pretty. Some smokers found their habit disgusting and clung to it out of need. The problem with Grace was that, if she was honest, she truly loved smoking. She loved the striking of the match, the first little drag that ignited the tip of the cigarette, the charge from the hit of the first inhalation, the soothing relaxation that followed. It was a small, sensuous pleasure, a cigarette, a private universe she could draw unto herself which was entirely hers. Grace opened her eyes, feeling a bit more prepared to face the day. Johnny was sitting on a low wall directly opposite her. Her heart quickened. He had shaved his stubbly beard. He looked good. She didn't need this.

"What are you doing here?"

"Well, I work nearby. And by the way, it's a free country. People can go where they want."

"So you just happen to pop up in my street?"

"I wanted to see you again." He spoke softly, solemnly, making it seem like an entirely reasonable desire. "There's a lot we must still talk about."

"What? Anything you have to say to me you can tell me right here and now."

He looked down at his feet and remained silent.

"It was nice to catch up with you, but we're grown ups now. We really don't have that much in common. Life has to go on."

Grace wasn't going to waste any more time here if Johnny didn't have anything to say. She turned to go. He stood up swiftly and blocked her path with his body.

"Nothing in common, huh?" An edge crept into his voice. "I see you, up and coming, office job. You forget where you came from?"

The accusation stung Grace. Of course, yes, she wanted nothing else but to forget where she had come from, but not in the way he was insinuating. She wasn't like that. Tears pricked at her eyes.

"Wait, wait. Grace! I didn't mean it. I just want to talk. Can you hear me out?"

Somewhere in her body, that body made up not of platelets and cells but of memory and forgetting, of love and the places that shape, a nerve jangled. She stroked the cross around her neck.

"I love you. I love you, Grace. That is what I have to say. You were the first person I loved, really loved, and I've always loved you. Not a day has gone by...And then seeing you again. Those feelings, right there, right here...." Johnny struck the place on his chest where his heart would be. More words fell from his mouth like unripe fruit reluctant to leave the tree.

Grace looked at him, really looked at him. His eyes were moist, his face red.

He loved her still. What did that mean after all these years? Sympathy softened her. To say it like that, to someone you didn't really know, must have been hard for him. And stupid. Another part of Grace delighted in his words. Had she not loved him too, every day, longed for him? Wondering and wishing, even after she'd given up waiting for him? Was that love? Or was it the remnant of that other love lost, so enmeshed with his disappearance: the longing for both of them blending into each other as day into night; just one gaping yearning for her mother and Johnny's return. Was this love?

"I loved you too, for a long time, Johnny." She sounded soft, defeated.

He lifted his head and gazed directly at her, the hypnotic eyes drinking and pulling at the same time. Much had changed about his face, but the long brown lashes, the inky stare, were as beautiful as she remembered.

"I wish we could just go somewhere and talk for a while, take our time."

"My house is up the road."

With those words, Grace knew that she had crossed every single boundary securing her place in the world. She was tugging away at the scaffolding of her life, and she knew it.

They walked wordlessly to the gate she'd left just a few minutes earlier. The street was quiet—all the neighborhood children were at school. If there were people at home, they gave no sign of it. Not a single car passed them, and if any lace curtains twitched as they entered the gate and walked up the steps to the front door, they remained oblivious to it.

An air of abandonment clung to the walls of the empty house.

Dirty dishes were piled in the sink, articles of Sindi's clothing littered the living room sofa. Johnny stood awkwardly in the middle of the room, looking unsure. Grace gathered up Sindi's clothes and gestured for him to sit down. He remained on his feet. She went to put the kettle on to make tea. From the kitchen she could see him scanning the row of framed family photos that hung on the front room wall: Sindi as a newborn, portraits of the three of them, a large confection of a wedding photo in a flowery frame. His presence jarred. Johnny was larger than David, whose frame was the only familiar one to Grace in this space. Johnny was broader, taller, and disproportionate to the room and the furniture in it. As if reading her mind, he stooped a bit to get a closer look at one picture. Grace brought the tea and sat down as a soft rain began to pelt the windows. As the house darkened, a sense of desolation crept over her. She felt like crying. She felt trapped with this stranger whom she couldn't let go.

"Well, all right. What else is there to say, Johnny?"

Wordlessly, he contemplated the question.

"Well, I spilled my guts already down there. Do I have to say it again? You like to see a man completely powerless before you, huh?"

The attempt at a joke fell flat.

"Yes, I know what you said. But now what? What is it that you want?"

He sighed. Grace noticed fine lines criss-crossing his cheeks, running up to the corners of his eyes. She noticed for the first time, too, that his eyes were circled by dark rings. He looked tired.

"I don't know, Grace. It's confusing to me. All those years ago, we were just children. But I loved you. You were something good in my life, something beautiful. And you loved me, I know you did. And after you left, after the thing with your mother, I was sad, bitter. I had lost a good thing in my life. I was back there, next door to your house, but nothing was the same. The cops, they kept me for ninety days. Nothing was the same after. I was never the same. I was broken. And I came back and you were gone, your mother gone. My parents were dead. I asked myself, why did I have to lose everyone I loved?"

There was nothing Grace could think of to say, so she kept

quiet and listened.

Johnny's tongue continued to loosen.

"And through the years I've thought about you, wondered. But you became unreal, like a beautiful dream that I'd had, something I could go back to in my mind whenever I needed it. When I was sad, hurt....I could go to this place that was you. You became a place for me to go to. I could feel better there. And then I saw you again. Just like that. Real. I knew right then that I still loved you. You were alive and...shining." He smiled at the recollection. "Don't laugh. It's the only word I can think of. You were shining with this light from somewhere inside you. I knew it would be easy to love you, because I could see you were still the same girl. You never really left me."

He was crying now. Grace had never seen any man, except her father, do that. He lowered himself onto the couch.

"Oh God, I know what you mean, Johnny. I loved you too, so much. I never said it to you then, and after, when I thought you were dead, I wished I had. But what did we know then? We were kids. But, yes, I did. I loved you. You were the one constant thing that kept me sane in those days."

They sat looking at each other, each absorbing the other's words. Having him there was like having a bit of her, Mary, with her, a part that Grace thought she had lost forever.

"I'm glad you thought about me too," Johnny said. "And to hear you say you loved me. That means a lot, even if it was long ago. I'm glad to hear it, that you've thought of me too all these years, Grace."

There it was, out in the open, an old love posthumously declared. A reciprocal love. And what could be sweeter than the delight of loving someone and having that love returned?

"But, Johnny, things are different now. Yes, I thought about you every day, but now there's this." Grace gestured around the room with her hand. "I have a family. I'm sure you do too. I am building something now, something I never had."

"Is he good to you?"

"Yes, he is very good to me. He is a very good man."

"Are you happy together?"

"Of course. He's my husband."

Johnny put his cup of tea aside. He stood up, scooped his

jacket from where he'd put it on the couch, and folded it over his arm. He said something about having to leave, and although Grace nodded, she knew she didn't want him to leave. If Johnny left now, she would lose him all over again. She watched as he walked toward the door. Her limbs felt like lead.

"Wait!"

She jumped up from the couch, reached for his shoulder, and pulled him back around to face her. He turned, pulled her toward him, and kissed her. She didn't resist.

This time there was nothing to break the spell between them. She kissed Johnny back with everything in her, every cell rejoicing at the marvel of his touch, the homecoming of skin on parched skin. Years, longings, grief melted away until there was nothing, nothing but a searing heat between them, burning them both until the edges between them blurred and disappeared. Johnny's body became a hollow into which she slid with perfection; he was a balm that erased every hurt and care from her weary soul. Grace allowed him into the sacred, unentered corners of her heart, and nothing else on the entire surface of God's beautiful earth, or below it, mattered.

Chapter 17

So began their affair. This was not something Grace had ever imagined herself capable of: the lying, the deception, the fabricated alibis that slithered off her tongue with startling ease. Yes, there was the big, foundational lie, but that was different. Her new lies required a constant inventiveness, a creativity and dexterity Grace almost admired in herself. At home, she invented a weekly after-work social, to which David encouraged her to go. Of course she felt guilty. Of course she hated the lies that slipped ever more effortlessly from her tongue. But not once did she hesitate when David asked questions about who was attending or what these evenings had been like. Her mind became a wellspring of lies. She found herself able to concoct the most elaborate stories. It seemed she had a penchant for fabrication hitherto unknown. It was such an easy thing to lie to David: she had, in fact, been doing it their entire life together.

It was wrong, she knew, but after a few weeks she stopped caring. Grace needed Johnny like she needed cigarettes. Seeing him once a week made her brighter, happier, more vibrant in other areas of her life. Having him back, knowing him intimately, having him listen with his attentive gaze to her stories and feelings; possessing him in that way had made her come back to life. The years without him she'd been asleep, she realized now, a somnambulist. Johnny had awakened her to happiness, to life itself. Feeling like a child again, Grace even caught herself skipping down the street one day. At home she was more attentive to David, more patient with Sindi. The baby didn't tire her as much. Grace felt more energetic than she had in years. She could even be heard humming as she made dinner or washed dishes. David noticed, relieved, and remarked at how well she was settling into motherhood. A false peace descended on their home. David was happy.

In these moments Grace felt terrible about her deception. The funny thing was that she didn't love David less after Johnny returned. Instead, Johnny had pried her guarded heart wide open, making it bigger and more capable of loving everyone in her life. In her worst moments, Grace rationalized it as good for her family. It was making her happy, and therefore David and Sindi were happier. Where before, she had struggled to relax and enjoy them, now she could fully embrace them with a healed heart, overflowing with joy. Johnny had fixed something in her. Something in that first embrace had gone "click," and the old stuff, the muck of suffering, flew out of her, leaving her light as a bird. She could dance around the kitchen table with David now, in the midst of the evening chaos, where before she would have brushed off his little gestures of affection.

Others noticed the change too. Mr. de Vries complimented her on looking beautiful one morning. No one had ever told her that before, not even David. It astonished Grace. She started taking more care with her appearance, choosing a new lipstick color and some fresh blush. She had never bothered before. Now she found herself before a fancy makeup counter at a department store in the heart of the city at lunchtime, where a consultant helped her find the best shades for her skin tone. Peering into the mirror, Grace saw Mary looking back through her eyes. So this was what it must have been like to be in Mary's skin; the admiring glances, the turned heads, the compliments and affirmations. Grace realized with a start that with her new look, she resembled her mother. Yes, she looked beautiful. For the first time, the memory of Mary made her smile. Mary would have loved this, taking her dull daughter to a makeup counter to try out a new look. Oh, Mama, why did you have to leave so soon?

Her hours with Johnny were never enough. They would meet close to Cape Town station after work on the designated night. Sometimes he brought his car, and they drove to the furthest beaches from the city. They couldn't go to the closer, more popular ones, for fear of being seen. Other times, they walked from one bar to the next down the spine of Cape Town, Long Street, which livened up in direct proportion to the day workers leaving the city. No one Grace knew frequented these parts, and there were enough little hole-in-the-wall places where they could sit, tucked away, drinking and talking. Sometimes they didn't even talk that much. It was enough for both of them to just be together, Grace leaning her head against Johnny's shoulder, or feeling his hand resting casually on her thigh in a gesture of possession. Sex happened in Johnny's car—always a furtive and desperate coupling that left neither of them satisfied, but holding just enough promise that the next time would be better. Grace disliked the empty parking lots and deserted beachside roads, but she couldn't stop. It made her feel closer to him, sealing the precious bond she thought she had lost forever.

They spoke little about their home lives. Obviously, Johnny knew about David and Sindi, and in the beginning he would ask after Sindi, but Grace always cut him short. She didn't want her child's name to cross his lips, and after a while he stopped asking about her. Grace wondered where he lived and with whom— they had never been to his home—and she remembered the woman who had answered the phone that first time she'd called. She had suggested that they go to his place once, but his reaction discouraged her from doing so again. Unreasonably, she was jealous of his life, jealous of the people with whom he shared it in daylight, with whom he could be and be seen freely. For all she knew, Johnny was married. He had said once that he wasn't, but she didn't quite believe this. And what if he was married? Would she have the right to be upset and demand an explanation? She, who was lying to and cheating on her husband—what recourse to morality did she have with Johnny? Grace decided that she didn't want to know about a wife, kids, girlfriends. When they were together, Johnny was hers, and she could stretch each encounter into a lifetime if she leaned in and turned her focus on him. Her soul, her mind, her body—she brought everything, everything into the car with her on their nights alone. She was present and attentive in the manner of a surgeon slicing through someone's life. If that was the only way she could have Johnny, then so it would be.

They spoke often of Mary. Driving around the upper contours of Signal Hill, the city twinkling below them, they would call her back from the dead and breathe her into the present.

"You know, I loved your mother," Johnny said one night. "It was like she recognized something in me, something good, that others didn't see. I mean, at first she was stuck up. Remember that first time I came knocking at your door?"

They laughed at the memory.

"If she'd had a gun, she would have fired it in the air to get rid of me. But once you got to know her...your mother was good to me."

"How? Tell me how she was good?" Grace implored.

She knew her father had liked Johnny and taken an interest, but Mary? She had not seen any explicit expressions of affection. Mary had softened toward him over the course of their acquaintance, but definitely regarded him as one would the help.

"Did you know she gave me a pair of your father's old shoes?"

Grace hadn't known that.

"Yes, she did. I had never owned a pair of shoes besides my school shoes until that day. That was so good of her, to think of me like that. She didn't have to do that, you know."

Grace smiled and fingered the cross of gold around her neck.

They sat in silence as headlights blurred into points of swishing light below. Grace felt she could have stayed there forever, in the warm car with soft rain tapping the roof and Good Hope's smooth love songs on the radio.

"The funny thing was, I never even wore them. Just having those shoes was enough for me. They made me walk a bit straighter somehow."

Grace turned and smiled at him.

"Your father was a good man too."

Grace started. They'd hardly ever broached the subject of Patrick after that first night.

"I know what he did was horrible, unforgivable. I can't even begin to imagine what that did to you. But sometimes people can do the most horrible things, things that define them for the rest of their lives. That doesn't mean that there wasn't some good in them. That doesn't mean we should forget about that good, the small kindnesses they showed."

Grace held his gaze. "Don't you dare talk to me about the goodness in that man," she said. "What do you know? Just what the hell do you know about living in constant terror, always waiting for the next blow?"

"More than you would think," Johnny snapped back. Grace

retreated. He was right.

"You should go and see him, you know," Johnny persisted. "You don't have to make him a part of your life. Just go and talk to him, before it's too late."

"What? What are you talking about? What do you know about my father?"

"He's out of prison," Johnny replied. "Been out for a while now. I see him sometimes, around the place."

Grace felt betrayed. Johnny had known this information about Patrick and he had kept it from her. Now he was urging her to go and see him?

"You must be insane!"

"He needs to..."

"What? What the hell do you know about my father's needs?"

It was clear to Grace now that there was some kind of relationship between Patrick and Johnny. She thought about the letter for the first time in a while. Unable to face its contents, she had locked it away in a little drawer at work. She knew it had to be from Patrick. Johnny was the only other person who could have written to her, but he had never mentioned sending her a letter so she knew there was only one other person who might have contacted her in this way.

Had they been conspiring against her? At this thought, Grace exploded with rage.

"You've seen him? You've seen that bastard?"

"Yes," Johnny said calmly. "He lives close to me. He needs—"

"I don't care what he needs. Did he care about what I needed? A mother—that's what I needed most. He took my mother away from me, and I will never forgive him. He took everything. I left there without any clothes, nothing. You tell him from me to fuck off!"

They drove home in silence. Grace vowed to herself for the thousandth time to break things off. Johnny was in on something with Patrick. Continuing this madness would almost certainly bring her father back into her life, along with a whole lot of explaining she'd have to do to David. She got out of the car a few doors from home, as was her habit, and slammed the door shut without saying goodnight.

But she couldn't stop with Johnny, no matter how hard she

tried. Every time they parted, Grace quietly resolved to stay away, that this would be the last time. She'd be strong for a few days but that familiar longing would form in her stomach, an emptiness that could only be soothed by him. Grace was in trouble. She was recklessly gambling with her life and the lives of Sindi and David, and enjoying it. Perhaps Patrick had been right, and she had been destined to become the slut her mother supposedly had been.

When these thoughts threatened to overwhelm her, Grace assured herself that everything would be okay. Hadn't she suffered enough in life, and wasn't she entitled to this bit of happiness? It was all right to steal some joy with him, her Johnny—he was her first love, and if the horrendous events of the past had not happened, who knew? They would probably have been together and married. If only, if only. Sindi would be his. That was how it should have been—yet another thing Patrick had taken away from her. The mess that was her life was squarely Patrick's fault.

Despite her resolve to end the affair, it continued. As their three-month "anniversary" came up, they looked forward to spending the stolen night together. Johnny had picked her up from work—a risky move—and they were on their way to Grace's favorite restaurant in Muizenberg, on the other coast, when the inevitable happened. Grace was laughing, happily chirping away at Johnny as they drove through the city, when they stopped at a red light. They'd become careless, daring the world to look at them, to find out. As Johnny turned to her, Grace leaned in and brushed his cheek with her fingers. It was a simple gesture, not overly demonstrative, but the kind of touch that signaled the sort of intimacy a married woman should have with no one but her husband. A playful, tender gesture at the end of a tiring week and the beginning of an exciting night. Her hand lingered on his face, and Grace turned to find herself looking into the eyes of Gwen, her mother-in-law, who had pulled up at the light beside them. The two women's faces froze as they recognized each other. No smiles, waves, or acknowledgments were necessary. The weight of Gwen's silent grasping of the situation filled the car. Both cars moved off as the light changed.

Nausea rose from the pit of Grace's stomach. She demanded to be taken home—Johnny, puzzled, wanted to know why.

"His mother, David's mother, she was in that car next to us. She just saw us."

Johnny grimaced, then tried to reassure her. They hadn't been doing anything right at that moment, had they? Nothing obviously wrong. Grace had told David she'd be out with friends. Could it not be explained in this way, that Johnny was one of those friends?

"Don't be stupid!" Grace screamed, tears streaming down her face. "Of course she could see what was going on."

Johnny's mood shifted from concern to anger.

"Stop it, just stop it, Grace! Stop crying this instant. You were happy enough to get into this in the beginning, remember? What did you think—that we'd be able to go on like this forever? This was going to happen sooner or later. And what kind of man is your husband anyway to let you go about like this, so freely, every week? Maybe he already knows. Maybe he's not man enough, or maybe he can't deal with this. Maybe he's relieved. Looks to me like he's turning a blind eye."

The words felt like a physical blow to the stomach. With anger rising in her throat, Grace cast a fresh eye on Johnny, this Johnny she had never seen before, who had never spoken to her in this sneering tone.

"I'm sorry, Grace, to be so direct," he said, and now his voice was devoid of malice, "but come on now, surely by now he must be wondering."

He had no business, no business at all to be talking about David like that, to even have David's name on his tongue. David, her good and solid David, didn't need to have his name besmirched like this.

"Don't you dare!" Grace hissed. "Leave David out of this."

Johnny laughed a shrill, thin laugh, throwing his head back in exaggeration. The venom was back in his voice as he attacked. "I have to leave him out of it? Me, who has never even met this wonderful man of yours? Who is the one running around on him? If he's so wonderful, why aren't you home with him?" Grace had no answer, except her usual demand to be taken home. They drove together in silence as darkness pressed down on the car. Traffic in the opposite lane whizzed past them, throwing erratic strobes of light onto Johnny's face, cloaking him alternately in darkness, then light. Now you see him, now you don't—a new game of hide and seek invented itself between them. Johnny lit a cigarette, passed it to Grace, and lit another for himself. Grace inhaled, picturing her carefully constructed life about to come crashing down. At this very moment, David would probably be opening the front door to his mother, happy as always to see her. He would have Sindi on his arm. Right now, he would be leaning forward to kiss his mother on the cheek as he always did; she would enter the house through the hallway, and in the living room she would proceed to destroy Grace's life. What a fool she had been. She wanted to get away from Johnny immediately, wished she had never set eyes on him that day on the train.

Johnny pulled into an emergency lane at the side of the road, snapped off the car's headlights, and with an impatient swoop, lit another cigarette.

"I told you, I want to go home," Grace protested weakly.

"I will take you home, but first, you listen to me."

His voice bore an authority unfamiliar to Grace. She blinked the tears out of her eyes and sat up, on guard. She was not used to this.

"Here's what we're going to do. I'll take you home tonight, but this will be the last time I leave you on the street. Tonight I come up with you, we tell David everything, you pack your bags and we're gone. You're leaving him—tonight."

"Are you mad?"

Grace was starting to feel afraid of this new, assertive Johnny, the one no longer whispering declarations of love but making firm plans. She had no idea who he was, or what he was capable of.

"Where's the madness in that? We can't go on like this. Let's make a clean break."

"What about my child? Have you thought about her? Where is she in your plan?"

His silence swelled like a fresh bruise, filling the car.

"I'm not just running off with you," Grace said. "I hardly know you."

"Oh, you knew me well enough to fuck me."

"Don't talk to me like that."

"Like what, the common whore that you are?"

The slap landed on his face before Grace knew what she was

doing. She wanted to say something to defend herself, but the words piled up against the inside of her throat, and her tongue became a dead weight. She struggled with the door handle in the dark, desperate to get away from this man. Johnny grabbed the fumbling hand, reining her in.

"I'm sorry, so sorry. Grace. No." He snatched both of her hands and kissed them. "I didn't mean that. It was just the heat of the moment. I love you, Grace. I want you to come with me. Leave him. We'll work out the baby somehow. Just come with me."

Grace sat back and leaned her head against the headrest. Johnny loved her. She could see it right there, written on his face. She could feel it in the grasp of his hand on hers. But he had called her a whore, the way Patrick had called her mother a whore, and later, Grace too. Maybe this was love. Maybe love grabbed ahold of you and made you so crazy that it wrung the worst shit out of you and made you spit it at the beloved if you thought they were leaving you. Maybe love did that to you. Johnny loved her, of that she was sure. She could feel it, and the rage happening between them was part of it. She had never felt this angry at David. But David hadn't dislodged her insides and rearranged them quite as Johnny could with just one word. This, here in the car, smacks and tugs and calling your woman a whore, this was love.

And she loved him too, more than anyone. Anyone except Sindi. She loved David, but in a different way. David was her rock, her best friend, but it had become like living with a brother. They were family and always would be, since Sindi bound them in blood, but Johnny—this was the kind of love that knocked you off the course of every known thing. It shook you by the shoulders and woke you up. To look at him was to feel again the course of long-suppressed love rush through her into a well of tenderness. Only Johnny could touch the concealed places of her joy and pain; only he was strong enough to bear these with her. He had relit something inside her that she thought had been snuffed out, woken a spirit that found itself soaring in his presence. She could not, would not, give this up. "Where would we go, if I left? Where do you live? I don't even know that."

"Look, you're going to have to take a bit of the truth here, Grace, to get to the other side, where things will be good for us. I've been living with someone. It's not serious. I never told you because it isn't really that serious between me and her—I was planning on leaving anyway."

Inside of Grace's chest, something splintered. The sound of blood rushing and buzzing dizzied her. Johnny had someone else. He had been going home to a woman, sharing a life, a bed with her. What could she say? She had known it, felt it, but hadn't been willing to face it. Now the fact slapped her in the face.

"Why didn't you tell me this before?"

"I just told you why...it wasn't important enough. You were going home to your husband every night. Did you expect me to be a monk? It was always going to be over quickly with her anyway. I can leave her tomorrow, tonight even. I told you, it's not serious."

"And then what? You leave tonight and then what?"

"We'll get a place together, you and me, Grace. We'll get a flat close by to the baby. You'll be close enough to see her."

"I'm not leaving her! I'm not leaving my baby. And her name is Sindi! You've never even said her name."

He punched the car window with his fist, sighed, and threw his head back.

"Calm down, Grace. Just think now, logically. We won't be able to have her at first. But we'll work it out. You'll have your baby. Think about it. A life together, out in the open. No more once-a-week, after dark. I know that I can make you happy, Grace."

He smiled and his eyes lit up. The lines on his forehead softened, and Grace started to feel better. He had come back into her life for a reason: surely it was no accident, meeting him on the train out of the blue like that? She hadn't even been thinking about him that day, and he came back. And weighing the two men, callous as that seemed, on the scale of her emotions, one thing was clear: Johnny was the love of her life. Once David found out everything about her—her father, her mother, the sordid details; Johnny, the lies—he probably wouldn't want her anyway. He would realize he deserved better. He deserved a decent, honest wife who didn't have a past life waiting to explode into the present. He should have a girl from a good, solid home who could match him in solidity and respectability. Not her, not Grace, born in shame and raised on a diet of humiliation.

Johnny knew all of this, and still he loved her. He saw all of her and wanted her. In him, her shame could rest and die.

"Are you sure you want this, Johnny?"

"Absolutely," he replied. No wavering.

"Are you sure you can take us on, both of us, me and Sindi?"

"Yes."

So sure and so confident: that settled it for Grace. He loved her. He loved her. He had come back for her, and he loved her. It was always supposed to be him. Fate had thrown a cruel twist into their story, and now they were correcting it.

They drove back to Grace's home in silence, having fixed their plans. They would go into the house together and confront David and his mother. Or, rather, they would allow those two to confront them. Grace would tell David it was over. She would pack some things for Sindi and herself—it would only take a minute—and they would go to a friend of Johnny's for the night. They would both take the next day off work. First they would take Sindi to daycare, and then they would find a place to rent. Tomorrow they would begin their new life together: Grace, Johnny, and Sindi.

They arrived at the front gate to find the house shrouded in darkness. Gwen's car was not parked against the curb next to the gate, where Grace had expected to see it. Surely she had driven straight to David, to share the news with her son? Gwen would not just have come and gone after delivering such devastating news. Surely not?

"Wait, Johnny. Let's just wait on this."

"What? Why?"

Grace felt her courage fading.

"Something's not right; it's not right to do it this way. I owe it to David to do it on my own."

"Bad idea. You don't know what he'll do. He might hurt you. Let me come with you."

"What? He'd never do that. He couldn't hurt a fly. No, please. Let me do this on my own. Trust me, Johnny. Let me go up there tonight one last time and tell him my way."

"Why? Now that we've decided, what could you want there?"

"I owe this to David at least. I know him, I know what to say. He would never hurt me. Just allow me to do this last thing for him."

Johnny's eyes darkened but he nodded assent. More words were exchanged, and he agreed to pick her up the next morning at eight. Grace climbed out of the car after an earnest "I love you" and slammed the door with finality. The taillights of his car were two tiny red pinpricks by the time Grace turned to ascend the steps.

This would be the last time she would enter the house as her home. Heavy of heart, for she had loved it here, but compelled by a force much larger than anything she felt for David, she made her way up. Not for the first time, Grace cursed God; a merciless, malignant God who took pleasure in shuffling the cards of their lives in the completely wrong order. This life with David was a mistake. As bad as she felt to hurt him, Grace needed to focus on Johnny, her first love. It should have been him all along.

It should have been him. The thought filled her head as she plodded up the stairs, toward the devastating deed she was forced to commit. It should have been him. The rhythm of her footsteps on the concrete veranda floor. It should have been him. The sound of the key as it turned in the front door lock. It should have been him. The scream of the stars, moon, and night sky retreating from her, as she prepared to do this thing, utterly alone.

The house was dark and quiet, save for the glow of a nightlight at the very back of the bedroom. She entered the living room. David lay sprawled there on the couch, fast asleep. The kitchen was neat, everything in its place, and the living room had been tidied. Grace slipped off her shoes and padded over to the couch on bare feet. She stood, feeling helpless, watching her husband in his sleep of innocence. Her heart swelled with tenderness for him, but she checked it, steeling herself. This should have been Johnny, right here, on the couch. Johnny should have been the father of the little girl asleep in the bedroom. David stirred, sensing her presence, and opened his eyes, soft from the memory of a dream. He smiled. Grace warmed to the crinkles around his eyes. He whispered hello in a sleepy voice. Clearly Gwen had not yet been there.

Grace sat down on the couch, on the spot he had made by moving back for her. How easily they accommodated one another —their bodies had their own language of give and take, each continuously shifting and making space to accommodate the other; each daily making way or leaning in as the other needed. Grace was about to shatter this bond; her heart had started its own personal excruciating breaking. Perhaps this would break them open to let the world in.

David reached for her, and she kissed his outstretched palm, leaving her lips to linger on his skin.

"I need to tell you something, David."

His arm encircled her waist, pulling her down. "No talking. Just lie with me for a bit."

Grace obliged, gratefully. A reprieve, ever the gentleman; even in this he was treating her softly.

David moved onto his side, making room for her. She slid in next to him, facing him, savoring the warmth of his hard familiar torso. Grace felt her muscles relax from the warmth of this body she knew and loved so well—every contour, every scar, every weakness. She put her hand, palm open, against his chest, and watched it slowly rising and falling with his deep, sleepy breath. She felt the thump of his heart against her hand; constant, steady, and predictable as the sun. This was the heart she was preparing to crush. Grace closed her eyes and let herself breathe the spicy smell of his cologne. Here she was again, under his wing. It felt like the most natural place to be—easy, comfortable. Here she was, back home, painted with garish makeup and stinking of smoke. She felt good against him, and dirty and cheap. He drew her in. She melted.

"I really have to tell you..."

Her hand lingering against his heart, in the darkness of the room, she tried to find his eyes, but they were closed. He whispered, shhhhh, and kissed the side of her neck. A part of her wanted to stay there forever, safe in his embrace with their daughter securely in the next room. But it should have been Johnny. She forced the image of the young boy with freckled cheeks into her head, conjured up the dark, beautiful face. She took a deep breath.

"It's okay, Gracie. I already know."

Her heart stopped. "How...?"

"I can smell it on you. I know you've started smoking again. It's all right."

Relief, then grief, flooded her body. Oh beautiful, naive David.

She did not deserve him.

His warm hands crept under her shirt and circled her breasts. His breathing deepened, and he pulled her toward him with a familiar urgency.

"It's okay, I forgive you." He smiled.

Grace was transported back to those first days under the oak trees at university, her longing for him then, the delightful discovery that he longed for her too, the friendship that had slowly built itself into something that all of a sudden, one day, became urgent. After weeks of looking and yearning: the moment when they both had to touch, to move into an accelerated realm of companionship that would blossom into physical love. Their first kiss one night in a friend's dorm room; their awkward fumbling becoming surer and stronger; the pleasure of his beard against her neck. Beads on the string that threaded their lives together. Her husband. Her baby's father. She saw it all: the wedding, Sindi's birth, the tired, sleepless nights that overwhelmed and dragged her into a chasm so deep, so empty, that Grace thought she had lost herself forever. David moved on top of her now, warm breath chasing her neck, while tears streamed down her face. He soothed, cooed, kissed the tears away while his hand worked surreptitiously to undo her skirt. She arched her body toward him, loving him with a fierceness that surprised her, wanting more than anything for this to be enough. She moaned, forgetting about Johnny, Sindi, her mother-in-law. For a time there existed only David. His body by now was naked, and she took in with him the final impressions of the last time.

It was the strangest sensation to one who had felt herself a victim all her life, to willingly inflict the worst kind of pain on one you love. Grace had gone through life blameless, believing that the hand God had dealt her conferred a righteous innocence. Yes, she bore that cross. She loved, she sacrificed, she did for others. She defined herself by this good; felt herself to be a special category of human being by virtue of the loss of her mother. She had protected those charged to her care, except for this day, when she would become the vehicle of destruction for David. Yet she had to do this breaking, inflict this pain, in order to be true to herself. She was sure that if Johnny walked out of her life she would die.

Grace lay with David, their limbs still entwined, and cradled him to her chest as she told him everything. Slowly, deliberately. She started with the day of Mary's death and ended with Gwen at the traffic lights. She made clear her intention to leave. She would forever after recall the heaving sobs, childlike, into her chest of the beloved face she could not see. And when he finally looked up, the light was gone from his eyes. To watch a life shatter is not easy, more so when you are the cause of that shattering.

David went and came, went and came, in and out of the room. Pleading followed questioning; bargaining followed pleading. Was she sure? He understood how losing a parent that way could fester, unresolved, and make her do things she really didn't mean to. If he had known, he would have supported her more, been a better husband. How terrible it must have been for her to bear this burden all alone these years.

He could understand, in a way, the thing with Johnny. It was grief, unresolved grief. This stranger had taken advantage of her, how was Grace to know that, blinded as she was by sadness. He could forgive all of it, everything, right then and never speak of it again if she promised to swear off the impostor. Grace couldn't. By the time light filtered into the living room through the cracks in the blinds, it was over, everything. A joint life, carefully crafted, lay tattered before them, and Grace could not help but wonder: was he worth this, at the same time as she reassured herself that yes, he must be.

It should have been Johnny.

Resignation settled in David's eyes. He asked Grace to leave the room so that he could make a phone call in private. A damp stain of fear spread across her chest. She left, slipping into the bedroom where Sindi was still asleep, blissfully unaware of the events that would shape the rest of her life. It was going to be okay, Grace told herself. David was angry and sad now, but he'd recover and realize that it was for the best. Who would want to hold onto a halfway love? David's voice traveled in a low whisper through the kitchen and bedroom. Grace couldn't make out the words, but she heard the sobbing, the breaking all over again. She stifled the urge to go and soothe him.

A long silence fell on the house, broken eventually by the fall of David's feet on the wooden floor as he moved toward the bedroom where Grace lay with Sindi. The digital alarm clocked screamed 6:45 am in bright red numerals.

"Pack your things. Now." He was calm, measured. "Be quick. Don't waste any more of my time. I want you out of here."

David threw a canvas tote at Grace, who unzipped it and moved away from the crib to the chest of drawers at the other side of the room. She pulled out some of her clothes and reached into Sindi's clothes drawer, but David gripped her hand.

"I said pack your bags." His face hovered close to hers and his lips curled back into a sneer as he spat the word. "Sindi is not going anywhere, do you hear me? Just take your stuff and get out! Now!"

Grace's courage sank to her feet. This was not how it was supposed to go. She reached out and laid a hand on David's upper arm to calm him down, but he jerked away violently. He clasped both her hands together and pulled her out of the bedroom. He never raised his voice in front of Sindi. He hadn't needed to before.

"David, I'm her mother..."

"Now you listen to me, Grace. That child, my daughter, will leave this house today over my dead body. Clear? You can go and be with the fucking love of your life, but you're not taking my child. Is that understood?"

"David, please. She needs me."

"Apparently not enough to keep you home nights. God, Grace, look at you. Look what you've become. Filth. You disgust me. Get out!"

"David, I understand that I hurt you..."

"Hurt me?" He laughed. The next words cut sharp and deep, mercilessly. "You rip my fucking heart out, and then you want to take my baby? Not happening! Now get out, before I do something we'll both regret."

Grace moved back toward the bedroom door, but David blocked her with his body.

"No, no, no! Not with my daughter. Get out, Grace! I'm warning you now. I've never lifted my hand to a woman, but as God is my witness, if you don't get out of my sight this minute, I will."

Grace felt the line that she could not cross, knew instinctively to push no further.

A key turned in the front door lock. It was Gwen, Grace could tell by the click-clack of her high heels.

"Coward!" Grace screamed at David, enraged and emboldened by Gwen's presence. "Calling on mommy to come and save you. Why don't you fight your battles like a man?"

David grabbed her by the shoulders, spun her around, and started marching her toward the front door. Grace screamed, and Sindi, awakened by the commotion, joined in.

Gwen was in the living room. She nodded silently at David, looking away as Grace tried to catch her eye. She moved past the struggling couple to go and soothe her granddaughter. As David forced her toward the front door, Grace could hear Gwen cooing at Sindi, comforting her. For once she had slept through the night, not waking to eat. She must be starving.

"God, David, she's hungry. Let me feed her at least!"

"No. She doesn't need you. We'll manage."

He unlocked the front door with one hand and pushed Grace toward it with the other. Then with one big, final heave, he ejected her from the front door, slamming it against Grace's breathless pleas. A few seconds later, he reopened the door, but only to throw out her handbag and coat. The door crunched again, locked. Grace rifled through her purse, searching for her keys—she was not going to leave Sindi without a fight—but David must have already removed them. With sweat dripping down her back despite the cold morning, Grace paced frantically around the stoep. She had lost all sense of decorum, all fear of what anyone might think: she needed to get back inside, back to her daughter. David would have to be reasonable. Words tumbled out of her, shrill and incoherent, punctuating the cold morning air. She heard herself shriek about lawyers, bastards, and bitches, while a small crowd gathered in the street below to watch the unfolding drama.

Grace looked down at herself—she was wearing the same clothes from the night before—so much for her emergency plan. David had not given her time even to pack the tote bag.

"What you looking at! Fuck all of you!" she screamed at the neighbors.

She went through her bag again and found a cigarette; lit it while she moved toward the front window of the house, trying to peer in. She found herself transported back to a spring day on Saturn Street, years ago, in another part of the city, when it had been her on the other side of the door, Patrick pacing the stoep like an animal. And here she was, years later, disgraced, retracing his steps. His words still rang in her ears—"Please, Mary, open the door"—and in that moment her hatred for him solidified and rose up through her, building into a full-throated, raucous shriek that ripped from her throat as it propelled her entire body—a ball of solid hatred—against the front door.

"Open up this door! I want my baby!"

Like pistons, her fists pummeled the wooden door, which refused to budge an inch. No one stirred inside. Grace remained oblivious to the growth in size of the audience down on the pavement. She didn't care who was watching, what they thought of her. She wanted her baby!

Johnny's car pulled up at the agreed upon time. Defeated, Grace made her way down the stairs under the collective gaze of the neighborhood and got in. Now they were really talking. They drove away—Grace crying, Johnny consoling—carrying the neighbors' judgement on their backs. Johnny promised her that this was not the end. He had a friend who had a lawyer friend. They would fight and get Sindi. Grace nodded, but doubted: since when did men who wore steel-toed boots count lawyers amongst their friends? As if reading her thoughts, Johnny withdrew his hand from hers and sped further away from the house that contained her heart, her Sindi.

Chapter 18

Grace free fell into her new life. Every tender security, every organizing principle she had clung to in the past to make sense of the world, was gone. She had walked away from the ritual and duty that had scaffolded her life, and in abandoning these, she floundered and flailed like a chick kicked out of the nest too soon. She had jumped voluntarily; no one had pushed her. But her newly won freedom swallowed her into a state of shiftless somnolence. There was work, which she managed competently, without too much thought. She made the journey into town every morning, as she always had.

Johnny found a flat in the suburb bordering her former neighborhood, keeping his promise that they would be close to the child she would never see. Perched in a Victorian building above a row of thrift shops, their apartment was small but sufficient. They furnished it with hand-me-downs draped with random bits of fabric, hung colorful beach wraps for curtains, and stuck candles in forgotten wine bottles. It would have been the perfect love nest had Grace been five years younger and unencumbered by motherhood. Her longing for Sindi throbbed like a toothache. Grace pined for her, wept for her. She took a perverse pleasure in the pain of breasts engorged with redundant milk, milk that eventually dried up to reveal a deeper, more devastating pain. She called David twice a day in a bid to see Sindi. She stalked the house overlooking the bay after work, trying to get a glimpse of them as they arrived home, but David was always ahead of her. He had moved the child to a different daycare—she had phoned the day-mother—and had changed her routine, while steadfastly refusing to answer the door or the phone. For two excruciating weeks after leaving, Grace lived without seeing her daughter.

This was not the auspicious start to a new life she'd hoped for with Johnny. For the first few weeks, most of their nights together were spent with Grace crying. Her lover reassured her that they would find a way to get the child, brought her little gifts of rose bouquets and trays of chocolate to make her smile. After a few days, these reassurances grew thinner and thinner until they shrank to silence when the topic of Sindi came up.

One evening Johnny said, "It's hard to see you like this, Grace. Can you try, if not for your own sake, but for mine too, to be a bit more cheerful?"

Grace glared at him for this suggestion. Johnny started reasoning that they should see the silver lining, that perhaps it was all for the best. The small flat was all they could afford, and it wasn't exactly suitable for a baby. Living with her father, Sindi had a bigger house, a garden, support from extended family. Neither he nor Grace had the grannies and grandpas to help with Sindi the way Gwen could.

Grace bristled. "You promised. That night in the car. You promised we would work this out."

"Yes, that's what I said." His reply was clipped. "And I would take her on if it was that simple. But he really wants her, and he's not letting go without a fight. And I'm not the kind of man to fight for another man's child. I would be happy to have her, Grace, but it's not simple anymore. Why spend money on lawyers, money we don't have? His mother has money—he can drag this out."

Fury rose within Grace like lava. Johnny was right, but to give in so easily?

She stopped talking to him about Sindi, but nevertheless made an appointment with a lawyer, who offered a grim prognosis. She had left the child, unheard of in most cases for a mother, and this fact, coupled with her adultery, would reflect poorly. David held the moral and legal high ground. It would be best for her to wait him out, let his anger cool, and then appeal to his sense of what was in his daughter's best interest. Grace argued, in vain, that David had thrown her out. No, it did not matter. Her intent had been to leave anyway. Perhaps he would become calmer as his anger subsided.

Adultery. Grace walked away from the lawyer's office with the word ringing in her ears. This was what she was now, an adulterer who had lied and cheated her way out of a perfectly good marriage. David had never hit her, had not ever had an unkind word for her. She was no better than her father. God knew, the way she felt these days, if murder would bring her baby back, she would unhesitatingly commit it. To live without her daughter would be a fate worse than death.

Grace resigned herself to waiting for David's anger to cool, sinking into her new life with Johnny. They both worked the obligatory eight hours a day, then spent all of their free time together. Unstructured by the demands of caring for a baby and keeping home, time took on an elastic quality. Days stretched out endlessly in the present, yet weeks and months contracted themselves into what felt like mere moments.

They did nothing much, really. Each was the only planet in the other's orbit. They'd come home, have a drink, cook supper or buy takeaways, fall into bed. They made love and spoke for hours, both greedy to imbibe as much of the other as they could. For the first time in her life, Grace felt fully understood. Johnny knew how to really listen, to ask questions that no one else had ever bothered with. They explored each other's minds and bodies at leisure. The space Sindi left in her life filled up with a love for Johnny that ran deeper and deeper every day. They went nowhere and saw no one. Slothful Friday nights bled into slothful weekends: lacking the structure of work days, Saturdays and Sundays passed in a blur of sleeping, drinking, and fucking. They would sleep until noon, get something to eat, go back to bed until early evening, and then venture out on the town. They frequented bars and cafés, always just the two of them. They drank a lot, laughed a lot. Nothing was hidden; everything was free—they flowed like wine across each other's jagged surfaces; soothing and medicinal. With Johnny, all her missing pieces came back together, rearranging themselves into some sort of a broken whole. Restored—that's how she felt. Nothing to hide. With him she could just be. If Sindi had been in it, life would have been perfect.

Grace kept trying to talk to David, but her old home remained barricaded, impenetrable, and he did not take her calls. Some nights, after dark, she stood outside the house, staring at the exposed window, trying to get the merest glimpse inside. Johnny was always there to hold her when she got back into the car, kiss away her tears, and tell her things would soon be better.

Her isolation deepened her dependency on Johnny. They spoke a great deal about family, the making and loss thereof. They had shared the experience of losing parents early in life, but also knew the power of being taken in and nurtured by people who didn't have to do it.

"I believe in created families," Johnny mused.

"What do you mean? All families are created. When a man and woman get together, have children—that is creating a family."

"That's not what I mean. I mean we choose people. Choose family. Create family in ways that have nothing to do with blood. Scrape it together. Like, even the riff raff, people you'd look at in the street and want nothing to do with. Even people like that. If you've both been thrown away, you can become a family to each other. I feel like you and me, that's what we are, Grace. We've seen the ugly side of life. That makes us family. Not a wedding ring or a baby that looks like both of us. You're my family now."

This made sense to Grace. "That's really sweet, Johnny. Yes, we've been each other's family for years."

They lay together in companionable silence.

"I'd give anything to see my parents just one more time," said Johnny.

Grace knew what was coming, but mellowed by liquor, she let him have his say.

"Have you thought about it, Grace? Going to see the old man?"

How funny that Johnny referred to him as the old man when, for Grace, Patrick lived forever as that robust thirty-something year old who had thrown her across the room with one hand.

In the intimate space of a late night conversation, had with wine in bed, it was difficult to be angry with Johnny. Grace listened without attacking.

"Why does it matter to you so much, Johnny? Why do you want me to see him?"

"For the reason I just gave you. I would do anything to see my father again, just for an hour. But I can't. He's gone. And once Patrick goes, he'll be lost to you forever."

"Well, your father didn't murder your mother. Maybe one reason why you wouldn't want to see him again?"

"I know, Grace. I know. I don't know how that must feel. I'll never know that. But you know—he's your father. And once he's gone, he's gone. You won't have the opportunity again. You'll never know why he did it, or what he's suffered with it."

"Wait, wait, Johnny. You know an awful lot about him. What's going on?"

Johnny didn't reply, but his look gave her pause.

"What? What is it? What are you not telling me?"

"It's no use, Grace, I can't keep secrets from you. He made me promise that I wouldn't say anything."

"What are you talking about?"

"Aah, Grace! I can't lie anymore. He's sick. Patrick is sick. He's dying. He didn't want me to tell you because he didn't want you to feel obligation. He wants to see you, but wanted you to come of your own free will, not because he is sick."

Grace had no words. She just stared at Johnny in disbelief. "He asked me to find you. That day on the train. It wasn't the first time I saw you. A few months before, I saw the place where you worked. I told him. He asked me to give you a letter, but I just couldn't go up to you like that, after all the years. I said no. So he asked me to follow you home. I got your address. He posted a letter. Didn't you get it?"

Again, Grace couldn't answer. He had seen her before? That day on the train she knew fate had brought them back together again. God had answered her prayers and brought Johnny back to her. But here he was now, saying he had seen her before, even followed her to her workplace and to her home. He'd known where she worked and lived for months. If she hadn't opened her eyes and found him in front of her, would he ever have come back to her?

Johnny, not comprehending her silence, kept on talking. "He's dying, Grace. Doesn't have much time left. He really wants to see you. Before it's too late."

"Wait." Grace held up her hand. "You lied to me, Johnny. You said you were always thinking about me, that you'd always loved me. If you loved me and missed me so much, why didn't you come to me the first time you saw me again?"

"What? I'm telling you your father is dying. Listen! We can talk about your romantic illusions later."

Grace jumped out of the bed, ready for a fight.

"My romantic illusions? You said you were always thinking of me! Always wanting to see me. Now I find out you lied. For months you knew where I was, could have come to me. Why did you wait?"

"I was scared, Grace."

"Scared?" Her voice rose in disbelief. "You followed me home! That is what's scary! You made me believe this fantasy of it being our destiny to meet on that train. You see Patrick all the time. You keep secrets from me. I left my fucking family for you. But you were scared? Scared of me?"

"Yes, Grace, I was scared. Scared you wouldn't recognize me. Scared you would recognize me but not want to know me. Look at you. Educated. Beautiful. A clever woman. What would someone like you want with me? I never even finished high school."

Grace melted. Yes, of course. She hadn't thought about it that way. Of course he would have been scared to approach her. She got back into bed. Johnny refilled her wine glass. She kissed the beloved curls on his head, stroked his cheek with the back of her hand. She couldn't stay angry with him. They had finished their bottle of wine before a subdued Grace asked: "What's wrong with him?"

"Cancer. Liver cancer."

"Is it curable?"

"The last I heard there was nothing they could do for him anymore. He was okay when last I saw him. He can still move around and stuff, but he's not going to survive this."

Grace lay in silence, digesting the news. Sharing the news seemed to distress Johnny—the two must be much closer than she had realized.

"And he's not lying. Some of the neighbors saw him at the hospital," Johnny added.

Grace felt nothing—not sympathy, not revulsion. A hundred more questions raced through her brain. Where was her father living? Who was taking care of him? Was he alone? He had loomed so large in her mind all her days as a killer, a taker of life, that she had never given one moment's thought to his mortality. He was vulnerable, sick, no longer all powerful. Finally. But the thought of his suffering gave her no joy.

The next day at work, Grace went straight to her desk drawer. She reached inside and her fingers felt the edges of the envelope. She tore it open and took out the single, folded page. It was covered in a scrawled, slanted hand.

Dear Grace,
I hope this letter finds you well. So many years have passed since I last saw you. I know there is nothing that I could possibly do or say to make amends for what I caused you. I am so sorry for what I did. I need to tell you that I am sorry. I think about her every day, and you too. This may be asking too much, but I would so appreciate it if you could give me the chance to see you. I want to tell you how sorry I am. You probably don't want to see me, but it would mean so much to an old man.
Sincerely,
Your father, Patrick de Leeuw

"Your father." Superfluous. As if Grace could have forgotten this fact. She read the letter several times, as if repetition would reveal some different meaning. Patrick was hardly an old man and calling himself such was manipulative, calculated to tug at the heartstrings. Perhaps being ill, he felt old. Certainly his life was coming to an end. Grace's thoughts turned to Sindi. She had not seen her daughter for two months. Was this excruciating pain she felt at Sindi's absence something akin to what Patrick was feeling? He could not possibly be missing Grace: how do you miss someone you don't know?

Grace could see how he could miss Mary. Maybe his longing for his daughter was something different. Perhaps it was a longing for a respite from guilt. Did he feel guilt? So many questions. Grace turned the letter round and round in her hands. The handwriting looked shaky. She tried to picture Patrick as he penned the words—at a desk? on his lap?—tried to conjure his features, but could not recall them. Right then she decided to see him, but only once. Once was more than he deserved.

She dialed the number at the bottom of the page.

By now Grace had got into the habit of waiting in the street every day outside the home she and David had once shared, on the off chance she'd see him. Eventually, her strategy bore fruit.

Grace caught him one night as he was scooping Sindi out of her car seat.

"Please can we talk, David? Please? For Sindi's sake," she begged.

He didn't speak, just gestured with his head for Grace to go up the stairs to the front door. Sindi gurgled at the sight of her mother, stretching out her arms toward Grace, who reached for her, but was swiftly blocked by David.

"Just go up the stairs, okay. Don't make another scene out here on the street."

They entered the house, an unhappy trio, and once inside, Grace finally grabbed her daughter. Sindi clung to her mother's neck as Grace wept. Her tears of joy, frustration, and longing bubbled up and spilled over into the soft creases of her baby's neck. Mercifully, David let them be. Once her tears subsided, Grace covered Sindi with kisses, stroked her limbs, and inhaled her soft fragrance. "My baby!" she exclaimed over and over. Sindi had grown so much—it had been two months since Grace had seen her. The child's features were changing. She looked more like Grace now than when she was born. David warmed up some leftover mashed potato and butternut squash for her, and Grace stood by awkwardly as he fed her. He was wonderful with her, always had been. Her absence had clearly deepened the bond between them. She wondered if Sindi had missed her. Did she feel the loss? She seemed happy enough here with David. Grace felt comforted by the knowledge that the child had recognized her, and was delighted to see her. She prayed that David would have mercy on her, that he would have a bit of compassion and give her at least some access to her child. Sindi needed her mother, as Grace needed her daughter. She couldn't imagine a life without her baby in it.

After Sindi had eaten, Grace and David sat down beside each other on the couch in the living room. They watched the baby crawl around the living room floor. She had started to stand up against the furniture, David explained, was walking around the room while holding onto things. It felt strangely familiar, talking like this, having David regale her with tales of the things she'd missed. They even shared a laugh as familiarity warmed the room, but then he became serious again and an invisible shield went up between them.

"So what do you want, Grace?"

It wasn't really a question, more an admonition to get on with it, state her business.

"David, I want to see her, I have to see her, regularly. We must work out some kind of thing, please. Not just for me. Think about her, David. Please. She needs a mother, she needs me."

"Well, look at you," he replied, calmly. "You grew up without a mother, and you turned out just fine."

Grace flinched, but remained calm. She couldn't afford to take this attack personally. She needed to remain focused. David was hurt and angry; of course he wanted to strike back and inflict pain.

"Yes, David, I grew up without a mother. Losing her was the worst thing that ever happened to me. I wouldn't want that to be Sindi's cross in life. Please, let's be adults. Let's work this out for her sake."

"That could have been easily avoided if you hadn't gone jolling around—" He was getting fired up.

Grace held up a placatory hand. "Okay. I'm sorry. I'm sorry that I lied to you. I'm sorry that I went behind your back. I was wrong, very wrong. But don't punish Sindi for my sins, David. Please don't do that."

David looked at his wife. "So let me get this clear," he stated. "Let me see if I understand this correctly, because you haven't yet said it directly. Do you want to get out of this marriage?"

"Yes."

"So you're not asking to come back? You don't want to give up this man and try again?"

"No."

"Are you sure?" For a second the soft eyes of the David she knew appeared from behind his steely gaze. "If you wanted to come back, we could put all of this behind us," he said.

Grace couldn't believe he felt this way, after everything that had happened. But she couldn't, wouldn't leave Johnny. They had lost all this time together and were only beginning to make it up. How on earth was she supposed to walk away from that? Grace shook her head slowly. "No, David. I'm sure of what I want."

They sat in silence for a while, David staring at his hands,

Grace at the floor. Sindi crawled up and pulled herself up against her father's knee, crowing and laughing. He picked her up, squeezed her, and seated her on his lap. She babbled cheerfully, while around them, the final ruins of family came clattering down.

"So, Grace, what do you suggest we do about Sindi? Surely you don't expect me to just hand her over to you and this stranger?"

"No, no, I don't want that. I've no right to ask. But we could share her. She could live with both of us, taking turns. Or let her come just for short periods to me. Please. I beg you."

David guffawed. A malicious, sneering sound left his lips. "No bloody way! That's no way for my daughter to live. Forget it, Grace. Forget it. I am going to divorce you, and I am going to ask for full custody."

Fear tightened Grace's chest. She had gambled and lost. Miscalculated. She tried to persuade David to at least give her some access to Sindi, but he became increasingly agitated. Grace begged; she pleaded.

Finally, David said, "I'll think about it some more, but I really don't want my child spending time with this man of yours. Now I think it's time for you to leave."

Grace had no choice but to scoop up Sindi and give her a final hug. She clung to the child, willing her body to remember the imprint of that sweet skin.

"Goodbye, Mummy's sweetheart."

She turned to leave, and Sindi started to cry. The child had no vocabulary yet, but grief came spilling out of her in the only way she knew. Grace shuttered her ears and her heart as she ran down the passage to the front door. As she closed the door behind her and descended the stairs to the street, her baby's low cries turned to a full-throttle wail. Oh dear God, what had she done? Breath itself escaped her. She swallowed an unarticulated scream that hammered against her heart: Sindi, Sindi, Sindi!

Chapter 19

Grace spiraled into joyless purgatory. Johnny did his best to cheer her, arguing that David would change his mind once he was less angry; that Sindi would not even remember this time of her life. But Grace, refusing to be cheered, vented at him.

"How do you know! You don't know David. You can't know that he'll change his mind."

"Oh for fuck's sake, Grace. David this, David that. You're right. I don't know David, and I don't want to know him. But I feel like he's living right here with us! It's all you ever talk about. David, David, David."

"Well, he's Sindi's father! He controls her now. It's up to him if I ever see my daughter again."

When the words "We could always have one of our own" escaped Johnny's mouth, Grace reeled. For the first time, she wanted to punch him. Disdain crept into her heart and made it a permanent residence. For this she had lost her daughter? A man who could glibly suggest that they forget about Sindi and replace her with another? Repugnance seeped into her words, gestures, and body, lacing every expression toward him with a cutting edge. She could not help it—as much as she loved Johnny, there co-existed in her body now the impulse to wound him. Johnny felt the chill even as she tried to hide it. They never exchanged words about this shift in temperature, but it was there, palpable, a pane of glass sitting between them that they could not see, but kept bumping up against even as they reached for each other.

Johnny started making detours on his way home from work, stopping off at a friend's place or for a round at the pub with increasing frequency. Jealousy made its bed alongside disdain in Grace's heart. After his nocturnal excursions, she'd greet him sullenly, if at all. Sometimes she'd pretend to be asleep when he got home, but mostly she'd wait, sit in silence, and watch him undress. She would lash him with her serrated edges when he tried to come close. Whatever had lived between them—love? lust?—became brittle. Their love-filled nights retreated into silence, blistered only by the occasional explosive fight.

It was on a night like this that Johnny hit her for the first time. She'd been waiting for him for hours and had found company and solace in a bottle of wine. He hadn't called before he'd left work, hadn't bothered to do that in a while. Grace lay curled up on a forlorn armchair, punctuating her swigs from the bottle with endless puffs from her cigarettes. The pleasant, dulling effect of smoke and wine had cooled the anger she'd felt rising earlier in the night, when he hadn't walked through the door at seven. This time, she'd make an effort, she told herself. She'd welcome him, smile, ask about his day; really ask, and really listen to his answers. She'd rub his shoulders, kiss his neck, soothe him with her words and body. But Grace fell asleep and woke hours later to a still empty home. Three in the morning. Where was he? Mouth dry and head throbbing, Grace had started to carry her body off to bed when he appeared through the front door. Addled with wine and sleep, Grace lunged at him. "Where have you been? Who were you with?"

"You're drunk. Shut up," Johnny countered.

"Not even a call from you—nothing!"

Grace pressed her face right up against his, rage oozing from every pore. She didn't see it coming: the palm of hand—wide, hard—the same palm that had caressed and held her, flattened into the side of her face. She lost her balance and staggered backwards, almost hitting the wall behind her. She brought her hand to her hot, stinging check, wet with tears, while Johnny looked on with wide eyes, his face immobilized with shock.

"How could you...?"

Shame veiled his eyes. Before he could answer, Grace ran from the living room and locked herself into the bedroom. What had her life become? Aunty Joan's voice rang clear in her head: swear to me you'll never let a man hit you. Grace had sworn. She would never be that woman. But here she was—how had she gotten here? If he could do it once, he would do it again. This much she knew. Shivering and sobbing, she pulled herself into the furthest corner of the bed, incredulous still that her Johnny with the kind eyes had done this to her.

Fear stalked her throughout the night. It skulked on the bed next to her, running its cold fingers up and down her back; came to sit at the base of her spine, where it mocked her: on your way to join your mother, cold and dead in the ground.

She tracked Johnny's movements, his every breath, in the next room; heard him pour some water, noted his shuffling up to the bedroom door and his waiting there, his listening. He didn't utter a word, or knock to be let in, just stood for the longest time. A predator stalking his prey. Grace didn't make a sound, didn't want him to hear her fear. Some men fed off fear: it emboldened them, gave them pleasure. She didn't yet know whether Johnny was such a man.

Sleep came to her when grey morning light filtered through the bedroom blinds. Sleeping fitfully, Grace felt her everywhere: her breath, her presence, rocking her into an anguished sleep. She was a sigh, floating over Grace like a leaf, but there, present: Mary.

Grace woke to the smell of food cooking and, for a dazed second, thought she was home with David. As she stirred, a cloud of stale cigarette smoke pressed down on her, bringing her back to the flat she shared with Johnny. Johnny, the boy with the dancing freckles and heavy lashes, without whom she could not live. And now the man who'd hit her. Perhaps she deserved it. She moved from the bed, body stiff and aching, and surveyed herself in the mirror. Bloodshot, sunken eyes looked back at her. Her skin was dull and grey, and lines deepened around her mouth. Twenty-eight years old. Her mother hadn't been much older than she was now when she had died. Was she destined to reenact the drama her mother had not been able to escape? She lit a cigarette and inhaled, watching the tendrils of smoke soften the image of the woman in the mirror. Her shoulders unlocked. Take a good look, she told herself. Who have you become? Motherless, fatherless; life about to be wasted. If only I still had my mother...the voice of self-pity droned.

But another voice, from a core of steel within her Grace was yet to find, surfaced, insisting on making itself heard. Look at the woman in the mirror, it chimed. Look! She's all you've got. You've got to hold onto her, fight for her life. Be your own mother. Save yourself!

There was a knock on the door. "Grace?" Johnny's voice was barely audible.

Grace braced herself, put out the cigarette and unlocked the door. She looked into his eyes, which were clouded with shame. They stood like this for a few moments, each on the other side of the threshold, surveying the other.

Grace broke the silence. "You hit me. You know me, know my story. You know about my mother, and you hit me." Her voice was flat and emotionless. "You of all people."

Johnny lifted his hand to his face, rubbing his jaw as if in disbelief; as if Grace was recounting a story about a stranger. When he spoke, regret came pouring out of him. "I'm sorry, so sorry, Grace. I didn't mean it...don't know what came over me..." The lines of an old, old song. "It's just, you were screaming in my face. It was too much. I know it's no excuse...I swear this will never happen again."

Yes, she knew every word to this song. There it was, the refrain. The it-won't-happen-again reborn, repurposed. A hand-me-down from a previous life being dressed up with a new bow. A second-hand gift from the man she loved. How many times had she heard these words from her father? Here they were again, the exact tone, inflection; the same guilty cock of the head to one side—her father's voice through her lover's mouth.

Johnny took her hand and led her to the kitchen table, where he sat her down. In front of her, he set down eggs on toast with a steaming cup of coffee. He had made a similar plate for himself.

"Please have something to eat."

Grace just stared at him.

"Please, just eat, Grace. Let's eat together and then we can talk, okay?"

She couldn't take her eyes off him. He was hungry and started wolfing down his food. It turned her stomach. He felt her gaze, looked up at her like a little boy who had been caught doing something bad. "Please eat, Grace."

Grace took a few mouthfuls of food, tasted nothing, and turned to the coffee. It warmed her, loosened her; the feeling began to come back into her shell-shocked limbs. She watched in silence as Johnny cleaned every morsel from his plate. When he had finished, he stood up and in one stride was at the other side of the table, kneeling at Grace's feet. "I am so, so sorry. You have to believe me. I would do anything to go back and undo it."

Grace shook her head slowly, deliberately.

"I don't know what came over me, Grace. Hell, I don't know. I've never done that before, and I'll never do it again. I swear, on my life, on my mother's grave. Never."

Her silence was an accusation that filled the air.

Still kneeling, Johnny buried his face in her lap and started crying. Great, heaving sobs wracked his body and traveled through hers, loosening something in her. She sat quietly, one hand still ensconced in his while the other stroked his curly head. After an eternity of tears they sat like this, his head on her lap, she comforting him, while each remained shuttered in their own private world. When all of his regret had left his body, Grace tilted his face up toward her and took in everything: his shock, his shame, the freckled face which had deepened in color over the years, the curls that clung to his head. His questioning eyes, burning with love. She felt sorry for him. This was the man who had saved her on that day at high school so many years ago, who had saved her in so many other ways. How could she have driven him to this? He had risked his life for her. This was the same man she'd sat with under the tree in her back yard as a child, the one happy memory of that place. He was gentle—gentle then and still now. If she had not screamed at him, provoked him.... If she hadn't turned her back on him because of the business of Sindi, this would never have happened. He would not have hit her. She couldn't really blame him for doing it—he had never done it before. She'd pushed him so far it was no wonder he had snapped. He was a human being, and she had overstepped. If she did better, stopped blaming him for the loss of Sindi, things could go back to the way they were in the beginning, when they had loved each other fully and without condition. Looking into his eyes, she saw all they could be. Love flooded through her: Johnny, her Johnny, who had been gone for so long, whom she thought had died. Nothing on God's earth and beyond it would make her give him up.

A quiet little voice cautioned: if he hits you once, he will do it again. It echoed and spread through her like a climbing vine, one Grace chose to clip right there, in the thrall of Johnny's pleading eyes. He loved her. For the first time in her life she felt truly loved, completely understood. Where David was safe and predictable like a mild summer's day, he had never inspired the feeling of wanting to lay her whole life down before him. Grace needed that tug at her heart; the turbulent, majestic drama of the summer storm she found in her love with Johnny. It made her feel alive. And here she was, embracing him now, forgiving all; more vibrant and alive than ever with her twin soul. She brought her lips to his face and kissed his tear-stained eyelids. "I forgive you," she said.

She went down on her knees to meet him. They embraced and tasted eternity with each other in that moment locked together. They renewed their love and themselves.

Buoyed by a new energy, later they left the dark flat and took a drive to the beach, where they frolicked in the surf like children. Afterwards they lay stretched out in the sun for hours, slipping into new skins. As the day ended, they bought ice-creams on the promenade and found a bench to sit on, where they giggled and bantered as they took in the salty air and the dipping sun. When darkness fell they remained on their bench, hand in hand, the sharp night air prickling their skins while waves lapping against the breakwater wall soothed them. Funny—as children they had lived so close to the beach but never even knew it. Patrick took her and Mary maybe once a year, if at all. Now, here it was, at their feet, and Grace felt like they owned it. Their own private beach. The moon shone only for them, winking through the clouds, blessing their love.

They returned home from the beach, relaxed and happy, to find good news. David had left a voice message. After speaking to a few different people, including Sindi's pediatrician, he had decided that Grace could have her for once a week visits. Grace howled with joy as she listened to the message. She flung her arms around Johnny and kissed him.

"See, didn't I tell you, Grace?" Johnny smiled. "He won't stay angry forever. He has to think about the child."

"Yes, you were right! Oh thank God, Johnny. Thank God!"

Yes, God was smiling down on them. Things were getting

UNMAKING GRACE

better. With Sindi back in her life, Grace would stop worrying, stop snapping. She just needed her daughter. She would stop being this bitch who made Johnny do things he had no control over. They'd save a little bit and then get a bigger place. This was the beginning of a new life. The terrible thing that had happened the night before would soon be forgotten.

After a quick call to David, they arranged for Sindi to come over the following Sunday. Grace flitted around the flat, unable to contain herself. She was going to see her baby again; she could hardly wait! Johnny would finally meet Sindi.

"Are you nervous, Johnny? Don't be nervous to meet her. She's gonna love you!"

"Why would I be nervous? It's a baby. It's not like she has a choice about liking me."

Such a simple statement, but it gave Grace pause. Sindi might be a baby, but she was a real person, with likes and dislikes. Johnny needed to be careful with her. But she said nothing, choosing to focus on the impending visit.

Later that week, Johnny came home with a tiny box of the type that sets women's hearts aflutter. Inside nestled a dainty ring, not the kind you present to a woman you want to marry, but nonetheless studded with three little diamonds.

"It's not much, not what I'd really like to give you." He smiled. "But in any case, there's nothing that can match the way I feel about you. I'll love you forever, Grace."

She had no words, just a smile and moist eyes for Johnny, her lovely Johnny. All the harm they had so carelessly inflicted upon each other (for Grace had now convinced herself that she was just as much at fault for him striking her) was forgotten as they kissed.

Chapter 20

The second beating was not so easy to forgive. After the first slap in the face, their happy ever after lasted exactly two weeks. Then another weekend came around. Johnny was out again, late; he arrived home smelling of liquor and perfume. Grace exploded. He said nothing as her insults crashed and bounced off him like big balls of hail. The longer he failed to react, the angrier Grace became until she ran up to him, lunged at him, and tried to force him to look at her, to look her in the eye and tell her where he'd been.

Johnny snapped. This time, the benign open palm was not to be. Knuckles connected with her eye socket, then went on to do their work on her lip, splitting it open and leaving a flourish of blood on her face. Grace retreated into the bedroom and tried to lock the door, but this time he came after her with a rage that had overtaken hers. He pinned her onto the bed by the shoulders while a knee pressed down hard into her thigh. She couldn't move, could not even scream. The more she tried to free herself, the harder he pushed.

"Now you listen to me, crazy bitch. I'm not going to take this shit from you. You stop this. You stop this madness or I will beat it out of you." The words hung in the air as he waited for them to have the intended effect. He was deadly serious, knew what he was doing. "I'm not a man who needs to beat a woman to feel like a man. But by God, you keep on pushing me, and this is how it will be. You push me up against a wall, and I will fight my way out. This, right here, is the consequence of the mess you made. You hear me?"

They stayed locked in this grotesque embrace for a while, him on top of her, both heaving. Grace closed her eyes, trying to get away from him and the angry hot breath assaulting her face. She wanted to die. Oblivion seemed the only way to erase the pain tearing through her. Then she went limp, and after a few calculated minutes Johnny rolled off her, sinking next to her into the bed.

Grace fought the urge to jump up and run through the flat and out the door. But where would she go? She was motherless, fatherless; Aunty Joan was gone. David, out of the question. She'd had a life, a good life, one she'd carelessly discarded. This was it, this room with its stench of cigarette smoke and stale wine, this was her home, her prison, the only place that could contain someone as low as her. Look around you, she told herself, this is where you belong; in filth because that's what you are. Filth. You made your bed, now lie in it.

The second time a man hits you, in the face, with his balled fist, there can be no more denial. Once can be passed off as an accident, a temporary loss of mind: he wasn't thinking, was drunk, was stressed; got away from himself. Twice? No. After the second time you can be under no illusions—you are inducted into that silent army of women. You see them everywhere, members of an invisible sisterhood of the downtrodden, their eyes vacant and their spirits sagging. Being one of them, you recognize them by the curve of the back, the stoop of the shoulders, the down-cast eyes; and sometimes, not often, the residue of a bruise. You catch the wounded eye on the train, on a taxi, and the moment of mutual recognition becomes the same instant in which you look away, ashamed. We are sisters, yes, but we daren't reach out to each other, and for heaven's sake, definitely mustn't talk about it. That would be betraying our men, ourselves. Shame settles like an invisible cloak around the shoulders of the sisterhood, impossible to shake no matter what they try. And after a while, as Grace found out, it becomes part of you—you believe you were meant to wear this garment, that you deserve no better because wasn't he the sun and the stars and the moon at the beginning? Didn't he love you, pursue you, adore you? Why would such adoration just go away if you hadn't done something to make it dry up? That indefinable something you must have done wrong, that made him stop loving and turn to punishing instead. It must be something in you; something innately unlovable or despicable about you to turn a man into that. And so you wear your shame, get comfortable in it, make indignity your home. It happens so gradually yet so quickly: the love that once lifted you tramples you down, and you start to believe that this is love. This is love. He hits me because he loves me. Loves me so much.

After the second beating, Grace could not get out of bed for three days. She lay there, stiff, her body bruised as if it had been hit by a truck. Johnny came and went as if nothing had happened. There were no earnest pleas, no rings, and no walks on the beach this time.

When he left the apartment, Grace produced a mirror from her nightstand with which to examine her face without leaving the bed. She stared at the woman in it for hours; the woman who looked like Mary on the day they went to the department store to get makeup. Grace stared through days, as the flesh around her eye went from purple to blue-black, and finally turned a sickly dark yellow. She would not be that woman who went to buy potions to hide the fact that her man had beaten her. Grace refused to be that woman, to have the glare of contempt and pity reflect at her from the eyes of strangers. Fuck that.

She called work and lied about having a bad strain of flu. Sindi was due for her second visit that weekend. The thought of David seeing her like this sent her heart racing, but she couldn't put off this hard-won visit. Sindi had come for five hours the week before. The visit had not gone as it had in Grace's fantasy. Sindi, afraid in an unfamiliar space, had moaned and fussed, refusing to leave Grace's arms. She was scared of Johnny and turned her little body violently away from him when he tried to take her from Grace's arms. Johnny had mumbled something about her being spoiled and left the flat. Grace felt heartbroken. No one had co-operated to create the cozy family scene she had imagined, and Johnny's departure had spoiled her reunion with Sindi. She spent the rest of her time with Sindi fretting about what Johnny was getting up to.

Grace thought about canceling the second visit, but now, more than ever, she needed the little girl. Her bruises were more or less healed, but she kept her sunglasses on as David dropped Sindi off. He stared at her, bemused by the sunglasses, and lingered at the door, as if waiting for an invitation to enter. Grace felt ashamed by her face, the flat, her life. She took Sindi and masked her embarrassment with rudeness, asking David to leave.

It was just as well. Johnny returned a few minutes later, and Grace was not yet ready for the two of them to encounter each other in her living room. She was surprised at Johnny's appearance, as he knew Sindi was coming—she'd expected that he'd stay away. They were still not speaking to each other. Each staked out a different corner of the cramped living room, Grace with Sindi, and stayed there. When it was time for David to pick Sindi up, Grace took the child down to the street so as to avoid the two men seeing each other.

There was another appointment, made weeks ago, that she could not get out of. She called the number she'd used before but could not get through. With just two days until they were due to meet, she had no way of reaching him to cancel. Of course she could just not go. She didn't owe him anything, not a damn thing! But even as these thoughts swirled around her mind, she knew that she'd be there, at the agreed upon place, at the appointed time. Was it curiosity? A need for reckoning? She didn't know, but even as she fought against wanting to see him, her compulsion to see him was stronger than any revulsion she felt. Some unknown force was propelling her toward the ordained time and place. Grace knew that she was destined to see him one more time—Patrick de Leeuw.

Chapter 21

Rows of identical houses whizzed past them as they drove through the township. The car was a warm cocoon insulating them from the dogs and running children, a bubble protecting Grace from the stares of strangers. Johnny and Grace had driven all the way in silence, cutting across the Cape Flats on the N2 highway. Her mood, already somber, dipped some more as they left the pleasantness of the suburbs close to the city. At first the drive seemed interminable, and then, once they arrived at the area bordering the airport, it was over too quickly. For the first time since that day, the day everything changed, Grace was back in the neighborhood where she'd spent her childhood living in that yellow house on Saturn Street.

"Why did you let him in?" she could still hear the voice, clear as a bell. The ringing had never stopped.

Here she was, several lifetimes later, winding down roads that were much narrower than she remembered: convoluted, labyrinthine. They felt claustrophobic. Nausea pushed up inside her as they slithered this way and that, circling narrow bends. Everything she remembered had faded. Paint peeled off walls, gutters sighed under the weight of years, fences had sagged and rusted. There was the shop Grace had once walked to every day for bread and milk and, when there was money, a small chocolate bar. It was still the same, just grimier. There was the shebeen Patrick had patronized. Here was the rent office, where the Casspirs had congregated in that terrible month leading up to her mother's death. What would have happened had Mary lived? Would she still be here, proud Mary, with her nose higher than everyone else's? How would she have carried herself against the indignity of the fading walls, the plastic bags flowering everywhere like sores?

And what about Johnny? Would he have been her only love?

She would not have had Sindi. But she didn't have Sindi now anyway, and she would not have known the pain of being denied her own flesh and blood. So many what ifs.

Memories flowed thick, like blood from freshly punctured flesh. That night when he came to the window, he'd wanted to see her. He had scared Grace witless, but she understood now the desire to see one's child, and how it could make you crazy. Had she not almost smashed a window of her own when David turned her out, and kicked and hammered at the front door with her fists?

The car slowed, and they came to a halt next to a curb. They had arrived at Patrick's place.

"You feeling okay?" Johnny asked.

She nodded. They were barely speaking, but he'd felt it important enough to bring her here to see Patrick. It would bring a sense of closure, might heal the thing that now lay between them too, he'd said.

Closure? Grace wanted to spit a mean laugh at that word. What the hell did Johnny know about anything? Maybe this meeting would make him feel better about himself, make him feel like the hero in orchestrating a reunion between estranged father and daughter. Maybe he needed to think of himself in those terms, as savior to both Patrick and Grace, since he was turning out to be one hell of a disappointment as a mere man.

"Wait here. Don't get out of the car," grunted Johnny.

He left, stepped through the gate of a forlorn greenhouse that had long ago given up the battle of trying to look presentable. An overgrown garden loomed up front, threatening to spill through the mesh fence out onto the pavement; the gate almost fell off its hinges as Johnny passed through. Johnny walked up the path but didn't stop at the front door. Instead, he turned right and went around the house, out of sight. So Patrick was a backyard dweller. What had Grace expected? A mansion? He was never going to come out of prison and own a proper house. A knot tightened in her stomach. In a few moments she'd be coming face to face with her father, the man who had murdered her mother.

There were still a few seconds of grace in which to duck out of the car and run to the nearest taxi rank. Yet her blood had turned to lead: she couldn't move; couldn't even summon the energy to roll down the car window. She focused on the gate. It would take maybe two screws to reattach the loose hinge and make it stand upright again, but with the decrepitude of this place, what difference would a functioning gate make? Where would one start anyway, on this house, so badly in need of repair?

Grace heard two soft voices and saw two figures come around the house. Johnny reappeared first on the narrow path, walking back to the gate, with a smaller figure following him. He walked slowly, pausing several times to turn back as if to check on a distracted child. While Johnny's confident steps fell on the path, the other man made a shuffling sound as he walked, as if he was dragging something behind him. Then they were out the gate, and Johnny stepped aside. There, right in front of Grace, stood her father.

Mouth dry, heart pounding, she took in the remnants of the monster who had terrorized her and her mother for so many years. He was withered, emaciated; thinner even than the kids running around on the pavement. He leaned on a walking stick, clutched with a gnarled hand. Johnny opened the passenger side of the door and gestured for Grace to get out. She moved slowly, as if weighted down by an invisible hand, until she was standing face to face with him, this man. Another shockwave passed through her body as she realized that she was taller than him. He craned his neck to look up at her, and there were those eyes, liquid-brown, moist and pleading. Pathetic. Look at you, Grace thought. How pathetic you've become. And how pathetic that this, this shadow of a man was the one who lived so vividly in her imagination, inspiring so much dread. To her mind he'd been a giant, a larger-than-life boogeyman who had taken away the one she loved most, and had robbed her of a childhood. Her whole life, he'd had this incredible power over her. He was the one she feared coming to get her; he was the shadow that haunted her nightmares. And he was this? Hardly human. The man who had beaten her mother was now a pathetic shell, wearing the haunted look of an abandoned child. She could push him to the ground with one hand. She could crush his windpipe under her thumbs without breaking a sweat. This was the monster she'd spent her life running from? This pathetic thing?

UNMAKING GRACE

"Grace." His voice was soft and raspy, struggling to make itself heard. "Grace, my Gracie. Is it really you?" Tears pooled in his eyes.

Oh God, not this. Not a tearful sobbing mess in the middle of the street.

He shuffled closer, eyes moist. The navy blue shirt he wore was new—she could tell by the stiff collar that chafed against his neck. It gave him the odd look of a tortoise that might retract his head into the shell of the shirt which hung limply around him. He was missing the entire row of his top teeth. Silver strands of saliva hung like moist cobwebs from baby pink gums, glistening as his slack mouth broke into a smile.

"Thank you for coming. Thank you. Thank you."

He bowed his head with each thank you, solidifying his gratitude. Grace allowed him to clasp her folded hands into his as his cane dropped to the ground.

"It is really you, Grace. Look at you, so beautiful."

Finally, the approval she had craved all her young life from him, coming now, decades too late.

"Thank you for coming. I've waited so long for this day."

Grace nodded, but didn't trust her voice to welcome this new father, the frail, infinitely human man, into her life.

"How are you, Grace?"

She nodded again.

"Please take off your glasses. I want to see you."

Grace pulled away and back into herself. Patrick stopped, waited. He had said something wrong. Johnny bent down to retrieve the cane and put it back into his hand.

"Thank you for coming." Patrick returned to his gratitude mantra, as if he did not know what else to say.

Johnny intervened. "Is there a place where you can sit down, be alone, Uncle Patrick?"

"Yes, we must talk alone," the older man replied. "But it's not good inside, not in there. Too much comings and goings. Too many ears and eyes."

"Let's go for a drive somewhere then," Johnny decided. Yes, he was in full savior mode.

Father and daughter nodded and climbed into the car. Grace, in the passenger seat, couldn't think of a single thing to say. Uncle Patrick. She hadn't missed the affectionate form of address. Her father and Johnny were close, closer than she had known. Perhaps this was what made Johnny think he could hit her. If this was his role model....

"Where do we want to go today?"

The false cheer in his voice sickened Grace. What was she doing here, with these two? She felt like smacking Johnny for encouraging this, for acting as if the occasion was a happy reunion. She reached into her bag for her trusty friends, and soon a soothing numbness washed over her and cigarette smoke filled the car's cramped interior.

"Can you spare me one, please?" Patrick piped up from the back seat.

"You have cancer and you want a cigarette?"

Grace regretted the words as soon as they'd left her mouth. There she was, cutting to the quick, making his devastating predicament clear. She had planned to wait for him to bring up the topic of cancer, and here she was, not even five minutes in, blundering around his grave. God, this was a terrible idea.

"It's okay," he responded cheerfully. "What's it gonna do to me? Kill me?" He chuckled, seeming pleased at his wisecrack.

Grace passed him a cigarette without turning round, and the smoke soon loosened his tongue.

"Johnny, there's one place I'd die to go, if you'd excuse the pun." Another chuckle. "Swartklip Beach. Do you remember it, Grace? We used to go there sometimes, you and me and your mummy. Do you remember?" His voice had turned high pitched and whiny with excitement, like a child clamoring for parental affirmation.

Anger closed Grace's throat. How dare he? How dare he speak her existence with his toothless beak. To bring up fond memories like this, like it had all been a lovely, gossamer dream, those years. How easily he spoke of her, without a trace of guilt. How unhampered the memories of her rolled off his tongue.

"Yes, I remember," Grace replied.

She turned her face away from him, but she was there again, thirteen years old, back on a day where the three of them had visited that beach. A year before it happened. Patrick and Mary had broken up for the hundredth time, or so it seemed to Grace, for real this time, but were trying to be friendly as a separated couple, for the sake of the child, you know. Of course Patrick's motive had been to woo Mary back. They had arrived at the beach, one, Grace remembered, Mary hadn't liked at all, but Patrick loved. The wind whipped sand into their faces, while clusters of small, jagged rocks, leaning into the sea at a sharp angle, assaulted the soles of their feet.

There was hardly any beach; getting into the water required pitter-pattering across the sharp, cutting rock edges. The waves beat against the rocks, stirring up dirty brown foam that flew up at them. Little droplets of spray clung to the air, lingering there and diffusing light. They were only going for a walk, a talk, like today, but Patrick, ever the water baby, could never resist the sight of the ocean and had to dip in for a swim. He stripped down to a pair of shorts, made his way through the jagged rocks, and like an arrow leaving its bow, plunged into the churning ocean. Mary and Grace sat on the beach watching his strong back recede toward the horizon, secure in the knowledge of his superior strength. His muscled back rose and fell, rose and fell into a steady beat, slicing the waves.

A few weeks before that visit to the beach, Grace had watched her father don a plain white robe and walk onto the large stage of an evangelical church—one of those tented ones that sprang up overnight. As the crowd cheered, she'd watched him step into a deep bath, followed by a robed preacher. The preacher embraced him and held him like a father holds a newborn, in a most tender embrace. Then he submerged Patrick's head under the water, holding him there for a few nerve-racking seconds.

"I baptize you in the name of the Father, the Son, and Holy Spirit," the pastor declared.

Patrick submitted. It was the first time Grace had seen him submit to any earthly force. Then he broke the water's surface and raised his fist in a gesture of victory. Tears of joy streamed down his face, mixed with the water of the baptismal font. He was saved—saved! He believed it; Grace believed it. He would never drink again, squander his money, mistreat them. Grace was ecstatic—happy for the new future the three of them would have together. Her father was now a man reborn, a man who would face the world sober, who would love her. They'd do father and daughter things like go for walks, sit on the beach. So far it had been good. Life had been good with this newly born man, this kinder version of his old self. Grace watched him cut through the water and smiled a smile that spread all the way inside of her, touching her heart in a way that she had not let it be touched by her father before. Mary had seen this Damascus moment too many times before to harbor anything but slight hope.

On that day, years ago, Grace had watched Patrick swim far out past the breakers and dirty foam, to the quiet calm of the open ocean. Once there, he stopped and turned to face them. Once again, a triumphal fist shot up through the water, puncturing the air with hope, waving at them, reassuring Mary and Grace that everything was okay. In that beautiful moment, the perfect conflation of all of their happiness, Grace caught herself wishing for a huge wave to engulf her father and drag him under. The thought had shamed her. She'd tried to wipe it from her mind, but it lingered. How beautiful and strange and tragic would her father's death be, right there in that moment of supreme strength and mastery. He would die young, at his physical peak. He would have been saved, in a state of grace, right with God. He would have died a kind, loving man who had taken his family to the beach one sunny afternoon, not the cruel raging monster they had known too intimately. Mary and Grace would have had the memory of him having been saved, baptized, sins repented for, and being new and happy in the world. His death, so soon after his baptism, would have provided the perfect arc to a brief, tumultuous life, finally at peace before its untimely end.

But Patrick had lived on, at the expense of Mary. He'd lived on to kill her. And here he was, asking with innocent wonder, "Do you remember that beach, Grace? Hey, Grace? The one we used to go to?"

She had loved him then, and now this memory of love flooded back. How tenuous and unpredictable is memory, a traitor sidling up to you, surprising you with thoughts of love for a man you have told yourself you hate. What did she feel for him now? As the outskirts of the town blurred and melted into sand dunes outside the car window, Grace scanned her heart. There was nothing. She felt nothing for her father: not hate, not disdain, not contempt. Even fear had left at the sight of him. All that remained was a cavernous nothing, an emptiness sitting in the middle of her chest where a heart should have been.

They arrived at the deserted beach parking lot. Grace got out while Johnny helped Patrick from the back seat, then walked over to her and whispered something about giving them some time alone. He climbed back into the car as Grace and Patrick made their way down a footworn path from the parking lot. Before them the beach stretched like a supple spine, curving in front of them, drenched with light. The sea was calm. Waves rolled in, spending themselves in foamy spray on the shore. Grace drank in the heavy, salty air and relaxed. She sank her bare feet into the comforting wet sand. Patrick hobbled along next to her, quiet, deep in thought. They reached a rock and sat down. Grace held her box of cigarettes out to Patrick, and they both lit up. She took a good look at him, for the first time, without flinching. A serene smile played on his face as he sampled the air.

"I love this place. It's a shame I haven't been able to come for years."

Grace smiled. Something about the sea air had calmed her. "You remember it, don't you? How I used to chase you around? I would let you get just far enough away to think you were going to escape, then I'd catch you and plop your little feet in the water, again and again, and you'd laugh. Laugh and scream. My little Grace. Tell me you remember?"

"Yes, I remember."

They sat in silence for a few minutes, taking in the vastness of the ocean, each in a capsule of private thought.

She thought again about the day he had swum out into the distance. It seemed like yesterday. And suddenly Mary was there too, her laughter just under the breath of the ocean, audible to anyone who cared to listen just a little deeper. He had swung Mary like that too, in the water. He couldn't understand them then: where he loved the sea they were both afraid of it, preferring land under their feet.

Grace thought about that day, the day her father got baptized in the tented church.

"So, Patrick, did you ever find Jesus again?"

"Jesus?" He looked bemused. "No. He left me for good after Mary....And good riddance. All my life, the idea of Jesus was used to punish me. The threat of him always hanging over me. He was a punishment, that's all. I learned nothing about love from those who said they knew him. Or about forgiveness."

Forgiveness. There it was. Was this his way of asking for it? She had come here wanting to confront, scream at him, tear into him. She had wanted this to be a day of reckoning, but all she could do now was sit and look at the shadow her father had become, and humor his trip down memory lane. Somewhere between the township and the beach, the will to fight him had evaporated.

"All these years, all these years, Grace, I've been praying, hoping that you'd have something good left of me, something of love to remember. I loved her, you know? I loved her. And she loved me too. I want you to know that. I was so scared that you'd think I was a monster. What you remember...I don't know..." His voice trailed off into insignificance. He tried again. "I'm not a monster, you know. I loved you both very much. I thought you would hate me, but when I saw you this morning getting out of that car, it was like she came back to me, my Mary. She was looking at me with your face. I knew right then that you wouldn't hate me, couldn't hate me, not coming to me like that, wearing Mary's face. No, you couldn't. Mary loved me. You know, she loved me."

He was talking more to himself now than to Grace. She listened, bearing witness to his great testimony of love.

"She was my Mary, and she was beautiful, the most beautiful that I've ever seen. And the miracle was that she loved me, that she saw anything in me at all. If only I hadn't tried to cling so tight. I didn't believe it, you know. That she could love me. And so I was always waiting for the day she'd leave. I was jealous and small. It choked me. I wish I had just loved her better."

A single tear rolled down his sunken cheek. His pain was palpable, engulfing Grace like the spray-filled air, clinging to her hair and skin. What about me, she thought. She had come here for judgement, condemnation. She had wanted to tell Patrick about her fucked up life, about the nightmares that still caused her to wake in a sweat, wishing for the sweet release of death. She had pictured him screaming, begging for forgiveness. Instead, here she was, listening to a soppy love story, moist like the back of the cigarette he was sucking. What about her pain? It dawned on her that her pain didn't matter, didn't exist for her father. She was merely a vessel, a receptacle for his.

"If you loved her so much, why the hell did you kill her? Answer me that."

Patrick fixed his gaze on her and held her with weepy eyes.

"I don't know, Grace. I don't know."

There it was. He didn't know why he'd done it. Wasn't thinking, didn't plan it. Just like every other time he'd hurt Mary. Tears coursed down his cheeks. For a moment Grace felt sympathy and wanted to fold him against her the way she did Sindi. But she hardened herself. He was pathetic.

"I snapped. I went mad. Honestly, I don't even remember. I just snapped."

She stared at him incredulously. "That's it? You just snapped?"

She wanted to scream and unleash the years of pain and longing for her onto his tiny frame, rain curses down on him until he broke under the burden of her rage. But with a hollow feeling, Grace realized that this wouldn't change a thing. He would never be able to feel her pain; he was incapable of it. Patrick's eyes told Grace that his own pain was so large, so all-consuming, stretching back so far into an abyss of misery that preceded her own life and that of her mother's that it blocked even the tiniest glimmer of empathy he might have had for someone else. In that moment, looking at his gaunt face, bearing his pain, clarity flashed through her. This is who he is. A mortally wounded human being. Something bigger than both of them, bigger than his drinking, had hurt him like this, had damaged him to the point where all he could feel was his enormous, oppressive pain. There was no room for anything else. It struck her like a gong. Anger fled her chest, and in its place came a deep sadness.

Patrick had looked away, but now he turned back to Grace, his gaze imploring. "Please take off your sunglasses, Grace," he said. "I want to see Mary's eyes one more time, before I die."

She smiled, sincerely this time. She moved her hands up to her face and removed the shades. Recognition jolted both of them, an electric current—him seeing her, his daughter, for the first time, fully; she, watching the reaction of his seeing, his witnessing. She didn't want to cause him more hurt, didn't want to wound. But through Grace's eyes, which were also Mary's, she wanted to see her father completely. She wanted him to fully understand. She had to press on. And with Mary's face, with Mary's lips, she had to ask.

"How did you become that way?"

His tears were falling freely, but the words could not come out. They were swallowed by the wind, the ocean and the sky. All he could do was rock softly back and forth, back and forth, back and forth, as she asked, again: "How did you come to be this way?"

Chapter 22

It felt like she was seeing the city for the first time: the day undressing itself, throwing off the garment of the blazing sun, the silhouetted mountain readying itself for sleep, the night sky glowing a soft orange. How many times had she stood at this window, dazed, mind churning, seeing nothing at all? Now she suspended herself in time at that magical moment between night and day, taking in everything—the darkening sky, the mountain bidding the sun goodnight, cars hustling the beams of their headlights down the highway. De Waal Drive, all lit up, sparkled like a diamond necklace flung around the mountain's neck.

Grace felt the city pulse through her veins. She was alive. She felt the temporality of all things. Instead of scaring her, it evoked a tenderness which nestled around the heart's cavities, filling the hollow places with peace. After tonight, this singular view of the city would never again be available to her. She would never see the mountain from this particular angle again, leaning over her like a protective aunt. She was leaving this place, leaving Johnny, and never coming back.

Turning around, she took in the detritus of their life together: the kitchen, dotted with mismatched cups and plates, the thread-bare loveseat hidden under a throw. In the next room the bed dominated the tiny apartment—so fitting. Now that compulsion and lust had slackened their hold, it seemed oversized, grotesque. The sight of it filled her with shame. Therein lay the cinders of her great love. Yes, she had loved him, still loved Johnny, but the curse of her father had seeped into their lives, obliterating every good thing between them. Barring the violence, they'd had a good thing. Love. The memory of that far-off place they'd both inhabited —their past. The ghost of her mother, compelling Grace to cling to him because once, eons ago, he'd existed in the same time and space with her, and Grace had loved them both at the same time. An intricate love bound with place and time, a love which gave her a history. But now it was time to go.

Mary. Grace thought of her in that ugly yellow house on Saturn Street. Mary would never escape those walls; she would never again move in the world beyond those confines. We all have our crosses to bear. Death was Mary's. Grace had tasted that freedom denied her mother but, unaccustomed to it, had constructed a familiar prison of her own in this dingy old apartment. She stroked the gold cross around her neck. If only she could reach back twenty years, take her mother by the hand and pull her through time, clear from that dark house as she walked out of her own prison.

It was too late for Mary, but today Grace was ready to fulfill an unspoken promise to herself, made on the day of her daughter's second visit to the home she shared with Johnny.

He had come in just after David had left, handing over a fussing Sindi. Grace and Johnny were in the middle of a cold war, the bruise around her eye giving just enough of a hint of what had happened between them the previous weekend.

Grace had spread a blanket on the floor and settled there with Sindi, some pillows, and the child's wooden blocks. They stacked the blocks, until nearly all of them were piled on top of one another to form a perilously leaning tower, which came crashing down. Sindi screamed and fell into a fit of sobs. Grace tried to comfort her, but Sindi's wails grew louder and louder.

"Make her stop," Johnny had seethed.

"I'm trying. Shouting will only make it worse."

Grace cooed and comforted. She scooped her daughter up into her arms and patted her back. Something was unsettling her so badly that nothing Grace did could console her.

Hung over from a night of drinking, Johnny lost his patience. In two quick strides he was next to them, and before Grace knew what was happening, he lifted Sindi roughly underneath her arms, plucked her from Grace, and took her into the bedroom. He plopped her down on the floor, shut the bedroom door behind him, and came back into the living room.

"What the hell do you think you're doing?"

Sindi had never been treated like that. From behind the bedroom door, her cries were building into full hysteria.

"She's spoiled, Grace. Never seen a child go on and on like that. You know, back at home kids don't even try it. They know they'll get the shit beaten out of them. You with your baby books. You with your airs and graces."

"But she's a baby. A baby!"

Grace rushed to the bedroom door. Johnny blocked her. "No, Grace. Let her cry!"

She couldn't calculate whether to take the risk. She left it, while behind the door Sindi heaved with heartrending sobs.

After a few minutes, Johnny could take no more. "This is not how I saw myself."

"What did you think? You knew about her, said you wanted her. I made it clear that Sindi came with me. Did you think she'd just be quiet and placid all day long? Babies cry, you know."

"Not like this. You've spoiled her. I can't, Grace. I can't see myself with this kind of a spoiled, pampered brat."

He marched to the front door, slamming it behind him as he left. As soon as he'd gone, Grace rushed to the bedroom and picked up her daughter. After a few minutes of soothing and then giving her a bottle, Sindi settled and fell fast asleep. The crying had exhausted her.

And then David's knock on the door; it was time for her to go. Grace had relinquished her daughter without saying a word.

"God, Grace, are you all right?" David had asked. She'd said yes, and shooed him away, embarrassed by the unkempt flat and her disheveled appearance. She hadn't even changed Sindi.

And that was that. She knew it in her bones. Grace could not walk away from Johnny for herself, but she had to do it for her daughter. It took another few days to plan her leaving without him knowing; to figure out the right time to pack her stuff and leave. To get a little room with a toilet and a hot plate at the back of someone's house. That would do nicely for now, just for her. Let the dead bury their dead, Aunty Joan used to say. That day, a week ago, when he had touched her daughter, Johnny became dead to her. No man would do to Sindi what had been done to her, no matter how much Grace loved him. She loved her daughter more.

It was time to bury Mary too, for good, leave her in the past, and uncouple her life from her mother's. It was time to forego the dance her parents had started decades ago, the dance whose familiar rhythm always beckoned and seduced. He loves you so. He loves you so much that he can't control his emotions. He loves you and so he hurts you to demonstrate just how much. He loves you and closes the gaping need of his love with his fists. He doesn't mean it when he hits you—that's the power of his love.

No.

No more.

Patrick had looked at Grace that day at the beach, and when he saw her face after the sunglasses came off, she knew he had recognized her beaten mother in her. He had stared for a long time at the bruise around Grace's eye, his eyes filling with tears as the realization of his inheritance to his only child sank in. He took her hands in his, the only time she'd let him touch her, and said: "Promise me one thing. Promise a dying man just one thing."

She had refused to promise, refused to give Patrick that.

"A man who does this will never change," Patrick said. "Takes one to know one. He's never going to change, Mary."

His memory was playing tricks. Grace said nothing. "Whatever's eating him, that devil riding him, is coming from deep inside him. That devil will lash you until he sorts it out for himself, within himself. Don't repeat our mistakes. Promise me that you'll leave."

She hadn't promised. She had had no words for her father and no desire to give him that as absolution. Let him find another way to ease his conscience. She hadn't given him forgiveness either —that was for another time, when her own wounds had been tended. It wasn't hers to give, and when she thought about it, he hadn't even asked for it.

From the window, Grace took in the mountain one more time. She had no parents, no family, no God. No ground to stand on; no one to lean on. Nobody to blame anymore. Only herself, responsible for herself. There were only the words of her Aunty Joan, resonant as the day she first heard them: "Never forget what you did today. You created something. Don't you ever forget that you have this inside you: the ability to create an entire universe out of nothing." Grace hadn't started yet, but ending this old life with Johnny was the first step to building one that was completely new. She finally got what Aunty Joan was trying to say that day on the living room floor, surrounded by paper and paint. There were still things to build, universes to make. She still had the most precious things of all: her life, and her daughter. She would steer both onto a different course.

For the first time, Grace was not afraid of life. She breathed in that mountain, and in it, caught a glimpse of what she could be like: towering, rooted and strong. Then she grasped her packed suitcase and, without looking back, walked away from that apartment and her old life. When the door slammed shut behind her, she knew she was free.

◆

ACKNOWLEDGEMENTS

I am grateful to the "village" that encouraged me to write and complete this novel. To Jennifer Bacon, who founded Black Women Writers, of which I was a member in Maryland, USA, and Shanna Smith, both sisters who encouraged and believed in me when I wasn't sure of myself—you are "a friend of my soul." Ranetta Hardin, Bettina Judd, Emily Bowden Cogdell, and Kellea Tibs were part of the circle when I first tested my creative voice, and I am thankful for their encouragement. The Hurston/Wright Foundation in Washington DC provided an opportunity to hone my skill as creative writer: I am especially thankful to have had as workshop facilitator, Tayari Jones, whose writing and teaching inspired and grew me. In South Africa, my creative tribe Diana Ferrus, Makhosazana Xaba, Patricia Fahrenfort, Nadia Sanger, Shelley Barry, Natasha Diedricks and Malika Ndlovu read and commented on various drafts, helping me craft a simpler, more stream-lined story. Thank you to the Department of English and School of Literature, Language and Media at the University of Witwatersrand for supporting my work. I am also grateful to Colleen Higgs of Modjaji Books, who took a chance on my work, and Alison Lowry, whose skill and sensitivity as an editor is unrivaled. To Vicky Stark, Rehana Rossouw and Julia Grey, who read and commented on my work: thank you. I am most grateful to my mother, Una Boswell and sister, Nina McKenzie, who read and commented on various drafts of this work—I am carried by your love and support.

Love Interrupted
Reneilwe Malatji

In her debut collection of short fiction, Reneilwe Malatji invites us into the intimate lives of South African women —their whispered conversations, their love lives, their triumphs and heartbreaks. This diverse chorus of female voices recounts misadventures with love, family, and community in powerful stories woven together with anger, politics, and wit. Malatji crafts an engaging collection full of rich, memorable characters who navigate work, love, patriarchy, and racism with thoughtfulness, strength, and humor.

"The stories in Reneilwe Malatji's Love Interrupted *peel back the gloss from atop South Africa's 'Black Diamonds' to reveal the sedimentary layers of truth in the lives of these model middle-class families: each story inventively unfurls a different desire, longing, or frustration. The stories of* Love Interrupted *are just like this, haunting you with their statements about the world of South Africa's middle class long after you've finished reading."*
   —Jacinda Townsend, author *Saint Monkey*

"The unsentimental style of these stories packs an emotional punch as they examine post-apartheid patriarchy through the eyes of various observant black women characters."
   —Foreword Reviews

"Many readers will see themselves in—and find themselves rooting for—the women in Malatji's solid debut."
   —Kirkus

We Kiss Them With Rain
by Futhi Ntshingila

Selected as a USBBY 2019 Outstanding International Book

A 2019 Skipping Stones Award honoree,
Multi-cultural and International Books

The terrible thing that steals 14-year-old Mvelo's song leads to startling revelations and unexpected opportunities. Life wasn't always this hard for 14-year-old Mvelo. There were good times living with her mother and her mother's boyfriend. Now her mother is dying of AIDS and what happened to Mvelo is the elephant in the room, despite its growing presence in their small shack. In this Shakespeare-style comedy, the things that seem to be are only a façade and the things that are revealed hand Mvelo a golden opportunity to change her fate. *We Kiss Them With Rain* explores both humor and tragedy in this modern-day fairy tale set in a squatter camp outside of Durban, South Africa.

> *"Taking place mostly in Durban, South Africa, the tale doesn't shy away from the reality of AIDS, poverty, or rampant sexual abuse, but instead of making those subjects its sole focus, Ntshingila folds them in with the other realities of life: love, joy, and hope. Ntshingila's lyrically wrought North American debut is a slim yet satisfying novel sure to trigger a wide range of emotions."*
> —Kirkus (Starred review)

> *"Those who appreciate realistic fiction will enjoy this novel in which young female characters learn to love themselves, no matter the circumstances"*
> —School Library Journal

> *"Full of heart and hope despite the emotionally challenging subject matter [...] A haunting, all-too-true story with plenty of compelling depth."*
> —Booklist Reviews

> *"It is a story about joy and hope and courage, and what it means to lift up others and be lifted oneself, and how one young girl found her voice in a world seemingly determined to take it away."*
> —Shelf Awareness (starred review)

Bom Boy
Yewande Omotoso

Abandoned by his birth mother, losing his adoptive mother to cancer, and failing to connect with his distant adoptive father, Leke—a troubled young man living in Cape Town—has developed some odd and possibly destructive habits: he stalks strangers, steals small objects, and visits doctors and healers in search of friendship. Through a series of letters written to him from prison by his Nigerian father, a man he has never met, Leke learns about the family curse—a curse which his father had unsuccessfully tried to remove. Leke's search to break the curse leads him to strange places.

"In this intricate and evocative novel about loss and separation, every character, exchange, sentiment and locale is rendered with due precision. Yewande Omotoso is a remarkably perceptive writer."
—Sefi Atta, author of *Everything Good Will Come*

"How did Yewande Omotoso pack so much in such a slender book? Bom Boy is a remarkable exploration of history and identity, love and loss. Omotoso's writing is honest, passionate and compelling."
—Chika Ungiwe, author *On Black Sisters Street* and
    The Black Messiah

"Bom Boy is an intricately structured literary novel that powerfully evokes family as a source of loss and struggle, but also of hope."
—Foreword Reviews

"Through three decades, two countries and multiple points of view, a complete picture of Leke's life in the present slowly surfaces in Yewande Omotoso's debut novel. [...] Despite his quirks, Leke's plight is curiously engaging as it speaks to the universal yearning to belong somewhere with someone."
—Shelf Awareness

"Omotoso's concise prose captures the racial complexities of the book's backdrop while enabling her protagonist to find his own way with her evocative plotting."
—World Literature Today